The Prisoner

The bomber was tumbling through the sky like a trailing comet, belching smoke and flame. In the clear night air you could sense the pilot frantically trying to right his stricken plane. But there was nothing he could do to save himself or his tail gunner.

Tom and Iris watch the enemy aircraft coming down towards the trees and make up their minds to go hunting for souvenirs. But they find more than they had bargained for: the injured pilot, tangled in the tree by his parachute. And then the air-raid warnings sound and they all have to take shelter. While the two English children and the teenage German pilot are confined together, with the bombs falling around them, Tom and Iris listen to Martin's story. They come to realize that the real casualties of war are not only the soldiers, sailors, and airmen, but the old, the sick, the women, and the children—and that bombs don't care what side you are on.

JAMES RIORDAN was born in Portsmouth and grew up there during the war. After he left school he worked as a postman, a barman, a crate stacker, a railway clerk, and a double bass player before doing his National Service in the RAF, where he learnt Russian. After demobilization he gained degrees from Birmingham, London, and Moscow, then worked as a translator in Moscow. Back in England he lectured at Portsmouth Polytechnic and Birmingham and Bradford universities and from 1989 at Surrey University where he is now Professor of Russian Studies. He has written over twenty academic books on Russian social issues and on sport, several collections of folk-tales, and a number of picture books. *Sweet Clarinet*, based on his own wartime recollections, was his first novel for children, and was shortlisted for the Whitbread Children's Book Award. *The Prisoner* is his second novel for Oxford University Press.

The Prisoner

The Prisoner

James Riordan

OXFORD
UNIVERSITY PRESS

OXFORD
UNIVERSITY PRESS

Great Clarendon Street, Oxford OX2 6DP

Oxford University Press is a department of the University of Oxford.
It furthers the University's objective of excellence in research, scholarship,
and education by publishing worldwide in

Oxford New York

*Athens Auckland Bangkok Bogotá Buenos Aires Calcutta
Cape Town Chennai Dar es Salaam Delhi Florence
Hong Kong Istanbul Karachi Kuala Lumpur Madrid Melbourne
Mexico City Mumbai Nairobi Paris São Paulo Singapore
Taipei Tokyo Toronto Warsaw*

and associated companies in *Berlin Ibadan*

Oxford is a registered trade mark of Oxford University Press
in the UK and in certain other countries

British Library Cataloguing in Publication Data available

ISBN 0 19 271812 6

Printed and bound in Great Britain by
Biddles Ltd., Guildford and King's Lynn

To Tania

I am the enemy you killed, my friend
Wilfred Owen

The first casualty when war comes is truth
Senator Hiram Johnson

Author's Note
I have based descriptions of the bombing of Hamburg
on eyewitness accounts and official records. I owe a debt
to the family diaries kindly lent me by Margret Pohl and
to Martin Middlebrook's *The Bombing of Hamburg*
(Penguin Books, 1980)

Contents

1	The Air Raid	1
2	Adolf and Winnie	5
3	Death	9
4	The Crash	13
5	HMS Barnabus	16
6	Searching for Wreckage	21
7	Finding the Plane	25
8	The German Pilot	30
9	First Aid	33
10	'My Name is Martin'	36
11	Rain	40
12	Interrogation	44
13	Martin's Story	47
14	The Jews	52
15	'Once Upon a Time . . . '	56
16	Catastrophe	61
17	'Why?'	67
18	Bonzo	69
19	The Firestorm	75
20	The Firing Squad	81
21	'Ginger'	88
22	Trapped	92
23	Grandad's Story	98
24	Flight	102
25	The Bomb	105
Postscript: Bare Facts		108

1

The Air Raid

The bomb fell in the middle of the night. Such a clear, still, starry night too. But this was wartime. September 1943. Adolf Hitler was at the door, pounding away at Britain's defences.

One moment all was as quiet as the grave. The next there was bedlam, noise loud enough to wake the dead.

The air-raid siren sounded the alarm.

Then an eerie silence. The lull before the storm.

Next came the distant drone of bombers approaching like a swarm of angry bees.

Almost at once the anti-aircraft guns started up.

The cheery boom of the Bofors guns merged with the death rattle of machine-gun fire. It was like the War God Thor running an iron spike across the sky's corrugated roof.

Another pause.

Then came quite a different sound, one which the ground watchers silently cheered: a flight of Spitfires thundering up the sky to intercept the foe.

Now began a desperate fight against time: to prevent the bombers releasing their deadly load.

But in the boundless night sky nothing could stop each and every German plane. The fighters might wing a Heinkel, even shoot one down; yet some always got through.

That meant the inevitable sound people dreaded: a bomb falling . . . and exploding.

It announced its coming clearly enough. But there was nothing you could do to stop it blowing you to smithereens.

To ten-year-old Tom and his thirteen-year-old sister

Iris war was serious fun. It was the greatest game ever invented. Danger made it so exciting.

Take the sky show. It was more brilliant than bonfire night. The two children would strain their ears to spot the different sounds.

'That's a Stuka divebomber.' (Tom) 'Must be after the ships in harbour or the radar masts on Portsdown Hill.'

'No, no.' (Iris) 'They do a high-pitched whine. It's a Dornier bomber—makes a noise like Grandad snoring.'

If the sounds of war grabbed their attention, it was the sights that exploded on their minds—like lightning after thunder.

The sky would come alive with twinkling shells and brilliant yellow searchlights, criss-crossing overhead. The white spray of tracer bullets climbed upwards, intersecting the orange-red flashes of salvoes from the ground.

It was so eerily beautiful against the backdrop of a pale crescent moon in a starry sky. A monster firework display.

If they were lucky, they'd see a direct hit—POOOFF! —an exploding firecracker: a red glow and cascading sparks, followed by a ball of fire spiralling round and round like a falling sycamore seed. They waited for the thud and mushroom cloud of black smoke as it hit the ground.

'GOT THE BLIGHTER!'

Never a thought that some poor devil was dead or dying, trapped in a burning plane or splattered in the mud with his guts spilling out.

Tom collected the names of warplanes like some kids collected names of motor cars—Ford, Morris, Wolseley, Rolls Royce. He'd made a set of model planes out of balsa-wood, paper, and glue. His enemy planes, though, were all of plasticine—because they were always crashing to the floor, downed by daring RAF pilots.

Tom's 'dog-fights' were set to special noise effects—buzzing and exploding mouth sounds that sent the two cats scurrying behind the copper boiler in the scullery. Even when he had his once-a-week bath in the zinc tub on Friday nights, he would perform heroic air-sea battles. Brave dive bombers were out to sink enemy U-boats (Camp coffee bottles) and battleships (empty Spam tins and bars of Lifebuoy soap).

Whenever he managed to corner Iris, usually when she was stuck in the air-raid shelter, he'd treat her to his war lore.

'Luftwaffe planes are dark grey with a black cross edged in white on the fuselage, and a black swastika on the tail. The Heinkel HE One Eleven is a dive bomber, just like the Stuka. Then there's the Heinkel seaplane, the Junker and Dornier Flying Pencil bombers. They're easy to spot from their odd cranked wings and flat undercarriages like coffin lids.

'Remember that; your life may depend on it one day. They're evil. But they're no match for our planes. Ours are brown and green with a red, white, and blue circle on the wings and sides. There are the twin-engined Blenheim, Wellington, and Halifax bombers. It's our brave fighters Hitler's most scared of—the Spitfire, Hurricane, and Hawker Tempest . . . '

Planes bored Iris rigid. She was more interested in exploring bombed buildings after the raids. You weren't supposed to, of course. But the wardens had more urgent jobs than keeping nosy kids out.

Iris and her best friend Maisie used to push open the door of any empty house and dive inside. Their hearts would be in their mouths as they linked hands for comfort.

When they poked around in the rubble, they half expected to unearth a dead body—or, worse, bits of bodies, like torn-off arms or bloody leg stumps. Up the rickety staircase they'd go in search of discarded relics—a dusty Snakes and Ladders board, a blackened poker, or a cracked picture frame.

Once they got a terrible shock. All of a sudden, they heard a rushing and groaning in the upstairs chimney, followed by a big crash. And a black, sooty creature with horns and tail landed in the fireplace. It was Old Nick himself out to nab them!

They couldn't get down the stairs and out of the house quickly enough. Afterwards, neither liked to admit it was most likely a sooty old rat!

Grandad once told her of a friend of his whose job it was to patrol the seashore—in case the enemy tried to sneak up by sea. He had to be on the look-out for anything unusual and report it—like spiky black mines drifting ashore.

'Well, see, one night he found the bloated body of a German sailor. It didn't half scare him. But that wasn't an end to it. Next night he was walking in pitch blackness along the shingle when someone goes and grabs him by the trouser leg . . . The poor bleeder nearly leapt sky high.

'Do you know what it was? A wee black and white terrier!'

2

Adolf and Winnie

Of course, war was not fun and games all the time. It had its down side. Wake up to the siren's wail, tumble sleepily out of bed, pull on dressing gown and wellies, and grab your gas mask. Down the stairs two at a time after Mum, with her urging you on, 'Come on or I'll clout you one. Hurry up, for Pete's sake!'

And sometimes the siren went two or three times a night! No respect for decent folk, those Jerries . . .

It was all right for Mum; she didn't need so much shut-eye. Yet even Mum followed a ritual before she left the house.

First came a frantic search for Adolf and Winnie.

Adolf was a half-wild black and white tom. His original name was Sooty; but he had been christened before the war. And once hostilities began, Sooty's nasty ways had earned him a new name. His evil consisted in hunting little mice and sparrows, and tormenting them to bits in a vicious game of pounce-go-pounce. To cap it all, he'd go and drop the dead trophy at your feet as if to say, 'That's my contribution to the war effort.'

Winnie took his name from our leader, Winston Churchill. He was a fat, contented ginger tom who kept aloof from all and sundry. Winnie was above scrapping with alley cats and would waddle around his estate like Toad of Toad Hall. If cats were human, you could imagine Winnie sticking up two claws in a Victory sign, smoking a fat cigar, and smiling smugly.

Winnie ignored Adolf unless that black Nazi crossed his path or tried to pinch his favourite snoozing spot. Then an imperious swish of his ginger tail and a low growl would send Adolf scuttling off.

5

Once Mum had gathered up the cats, she took three precious items from the kitchen: the ration books, a 'lucky' horseshoe, and a chipped china chamber pot.

Mum was very particular about 'spending a penny', not to mention 'tuppence'. The lavatory was outdoors, almost within weeing distance of the shelter, but for some reason she was scared of the children being caught with their pants down.

'What if a bomb dropped and the neighbours found you like that in the lav!' she'd go on. 'I'd never live it down.'

It was the same with underwear. If there was a raid on, the children would have to be wearing clean vest, pants, or knickers—just in case they ended up in hospital and got stripped down to their undies.

The last item for the shelter was a plentiful supply of dry newspaper—'for emergencies'.

As for the children, their one essential piece of equipment was the dreaded gas mask. Everyone had to wear one. Babies had gas masks, horses had gas masks, grown-ups had gas masks, and kids had gas masks. You had to carry them in a clumsy metal case slung over your shoulder every time you went out. And they were the last thing you grabbed before diving into the shelter.

Tom and Iris never stopped poking fun at each other in their gas masks.

'You look like Mickey Mouse,' Tom used to tell his sister in a muffled voice through the elephant trunk of a sound box.

'And you're an ant-eater in pyjamas,' she'd mutter back.

Funny thing was they'd never experienced gas. Hitler was probably scared of dropping any gas in case he got gassed back. But there were plenty of old men about—wheezing witness to the horrible effects of gas in World War I.

Everyone in the same row of houses as Tom and Iris had their back-garden Anderson Shelter. When war broke out, Dad had dug a big hole in the ground—exactly three feet deep, according to War Ministry instructions. Men in lorries had delivered metal sheets of corrugated iron which Dad had slotted into the sides of the hole.

The sheets arched over to make a roof, bolted in the middle. Then Mum hung a thick brown blanket over the door—you weren't allowed wood for fear of splinters when bombs fell. The whole family rigged up a couple of bunks with blankets and lino—'as snug as a bug in a rug', as Mum put it.

Was it heck! What everyone forgot was the rain. Whenever it rained, water sloshed down into the shelter and made it stink to high heaven. The family did their best to bail out, but it was a losing battle. It must have been the fault of all those planes diving in and out of rain clouds, upsetting the Rain God. It came down cats and dogs.

Round the sides of the shelter were sandbags soaked in creosote to stop wet soil rotting the sacking. And when it rained, the smell was strong enough to get you hooked on the stuff.

Like most families, Tom and Iris's kept rabbits. They were housed in hutches at the end of the garden. It was the children's job to go collecting rabbit food in the fields and woods—dandelion leaves, burdock, and 'lamb's tails', any sort of greens, including farmers' cabbages and Brussels sprouts! But Mum also fed them on potato peelings which she softened up in the oven.

One night, after the siren went and Mum, Iris, and Tom were sitting in the shelter with shells and shrapnel showering down, Mum suddenly gave a yelp.

'Crikey! I've left the peelings in the oven.'

'Never mind, Mum,' said Iris. 'The rabbits won't starve overnight.'

7

'Blow the rabbits,' said Mum in a tizzy. 'The whole house could go up in smoke!'

Hitler wasn't going to stop her dashing back indoors to switch off the oven. Up she jumped and made a run for the house, hands covering her head like an umbrella—in case a bomb fell. A few minutes later she was back with a tray of smoking peelings in her hands.

For the rest of the alert, the children had to put up with the stink of burnt potato peel in the cramped shelter.

If only Hitler knew the lengths people went to in order to win the war.

3

Death

War could be cruel. Although no gas fell from the skies, bombs did.

Dive bombs.

Blast bombs.

Flying bombs.

Fire bombs.

Incendiaries.

Tom and Iris well remembered the time, six months before, when death came into their young lives. They had sat with Mum in the shelter. And it had been a long, tiring, boring night. They were expecting the All-Clear at any moment when they caught the ominous sound of an engine overhead: putt-putt-putt-putt.

All at once, the 'putting' cut out; the children's eyes grew wide with fear and, automatically, they began to count out loud:

'One, two, three, four, five, six . . . '

They knew from experience what to expect. The explosion came dead on the count of six.

The bang was so close it blocked their ears—like water does when you dive into the sea. In the awful lull that followed, no one in the shelter spoke until the All-Clear sounded. They all breathed out heavily after holding their breath.

'Someone's copped it,' said Mum quietly.

She was right.

It was poor Mr and Mrs Brickwood who owned the corner shop. As Iris and Tom emerged from the shelter they could smell cordite in the early morning air; it was mixed with the dust of fallen bricks. And they could see

a pall of spiralling smoke rising above the next terrace—
Ernest Street.

'Come on, let's see if we can lend a hand,' said Mum,
taking their arms and pulling them towards the dusty
smoke.

The road and pavement were littered with grey roof
slates, broken glass, and smoking brick rubble. The
bedroom wall above the corner shop was missing. It
seemed rude to peer into something as intimate as a
bedroom. Not that anyone was still in bed.

The children squinted up curiously. They could see a
picture of the king hanging lopsidedly on one wall.
Despite the ruins all about him, King George was still
smiling shyly. In the space where the outside wall
should have been was an iron bed, its back legs
dangling over the edge, swaying to and fro in the
morning breeze.

Mum and the two children, still holding hands, looked
on as ARP wardens in white tin hats dug with bare
hands in the ground floor ruins of what was once a tidy
family shop. Amidst the spilled groceries and cigarettes
and scattered flour and sugar, they spotted dusty
clothing and broken china ornaments that had evidently
fallen through the hole in the ceiling.

Bottles of brown vinegar had smashed, leaving a sour,
sharp smell in the road, like smelling salts.

A lonely pair of spectacles lay in the roadway, one
eyeglass cracked, the other squinting like an angry eyeball
in the sunshine. They belonged to Mr Brickwood.

It was not long before two stretchers were being lifted
towards an ambulance; they were covered in khaki
blankets with red stripes down the side. The blankets
did not conceal the bodies entirely. Unsightly grey legs
poked out at one end.

One pair of feet was clad in brown slippers, the other
was naked, its ugly toes erect like miniature tombstones.

The Brickwoods were the first war victims the

children had ever seen. And they both felt sad for
having known the dead. Mr Brickwood was ever such a
nice man, often slipping a stick of barley sugar or a
couple of red aniseed balls into the week's groceries.
'For the kiddies,' he'd say with a wink.

True, his wife could be a bit standoffish when the
mood took her.

That morning of death stuck in their minds a long
time for another reason. In next to no time the entire
street was out, pitching in, digging for precious
belongings in the rubble—maybe the Brickwood cat
still had eight lives left if found. Elderly men, teenagers,
mothers with little children were all doing their bit,
assisting as best they could.

War had barged into their community, touched them
all, killed a friend. That made it personal.

Women in flowery pinnies bustled out of doors with
endless cups of tea and cocoa for the delvers and
diggers, and the old folk in shock.

From out of nowhere a bushy-bearded fellow
appeared with an accordion strapped to his chest. He
sat down on a wooden chair in the centre of the road and
set to serenading the searchers.

'It's a long way to Tipperary . . . '

'There'll always be an England . . . '

'Roll out the barrel . . . '

Now and then he'd sing a song not meant for tender
ears, to the tune of 'Colonel Bogey'.

No one minded. It helped them pack up their
troubles, forget for a moment the terrible fate of the
Brickwoods.

Another remarkable thing. No one tried to pinch the
food scattered all over the road. That was unthinkable.
They would all take their due from ration cards. Not a
crumb more, thank you very much.

'That bomb must have had the Brickwood name on
it,' Tom and Iris heard a neighbour say.

They wondered what that meant. Did the Germans have bombs for everyone? With their names written on them? How cunning they were!

Six months after the Brickwood bomb, another 'nuisance' bomb fell, this time on St Swithun's Church across the road from their house. As luck would have it, the old vicar was snoring blissfully in the rectory on the edge of town.

Normally, the dockyard was the prime target, yet every so often planes dumped bombs any old where before flying off home.

Even though it may have had his name on it, the 'dump' bomb failed to find the vicar. No one was hurt. But the blast blew out the windows of nearby houses and knocked half the slates off the roofs. Tom and Iris were in for a draughty time.

They weren't to know it then, but that bomb definitely had *their* names written on it: IRIS and TOM.

4

The Crash

From the safety of their shelter, the children watched the 'dog fight' beneath the stars.

Spitfires v. Messerschmitts.

Searchlights were sweeping the sky like cinema torches at the Tivoli. Puffs of orange and red smoke lit up the heavens as shells exploded about the planes. All the while, the dark, sinister shapes of bombers ducked and dived—and sometimes spiralled to the ground trailing fire and smoke.

It was hard to tell which was which. Ours or theirs.

Then, all at once, the children saw a big bomber separated from the German squadron by chasing fighters; they were moving in for the kill. It was like lionesses hunting a herd of buffalo and trapping one great wide-eyed beast.

The German pilot was flying for his life, so low you could have hit him with a shotgun. Red flickering fire was spitting from the tail gun, but the swift Spitfires were much too nifty for him. They seemed to taunt and harry the helpless pilot until, disheartened, he gave up the fight.

Suddenly, the lead Spitfire darted in for the kill, firing from both wing guns into the dark hull of the enemy plane.

'Got him!' yelled Iris. 'Serves the beggar right for smashing our windows.'

Sure enough, the bomber was tumbling through the sky like a trailing comet, belching smoke and flame. In the clear night air you could sense the pilot frantically trying to right his stricken plane. But there was nothing he could do to save himself or his tail gunner.

Tom was more concerned for the men than the plane.

'Why don't they bail out?' he asked anxiously.

'Maybe they're strapped in,' said Iris. 'Good riddance to bad rubbish, if you ask me. That's two Germans less.'

She strained her eyes through the clouded windows of her gas mask. And slowly the smile on her face faded to a frown.

'Hold on, what's that?'

She fancied she spotted a parachute floating down in the wake of the nosediving plane. But she quickly put it out of mind. For all at once she realized the danger they were in. The blazing wreck appeared to be heading for their terrace of houses.

Yet then, to her relief, she saw it veer away and plunge towards the tree-fringed clay pits a mile or so away.

It all seemed to happen in slow motion. The black, cigar-shaped aircraft twisted and turned desperately in its death throes. It was like a bird thrashing about on one wing.

The children followed the plane's descent, listening to its high-pitched scream, until it disappeared over the rooftops. Shortly after, they heard a big bang; the shelter shuddered and a black plume of smoke billowed high into the sky from the old clay pits.

Iris clapped her hands with glee.

'That's deaded him!' she yelled at the top of her voice.

Tom wasn't so happy.

'What a horrible way to die,' he said.

Iris's big glass eyes glared at her little brother.

'It was him or us,' she squawked through her gas mask. 'He would have blown us to Kingdom Come without blinking.'

'That's war for you,' Mum muttered absently. After a pause, she added sadly, 'I don't suppose anyone over there grieved when your dad's ship went down.'

14

Mention of Dad changed the mood in the shelter straightaway. Their thoughts abruptly switched from the skies to the cold cruel sea.

5

HMS Barnabus

Able Seaman William Turner had served aboard HMS Barnabus. The destroyer had sailed out of Portsmouth through the Solent in early 1940. She had set course for the Atlantic, aiming to reach North Africa by spring. Of course, she had to run the gauntlet of enemy submarines and warplanes. It was a dodgy run.

She had only made it to the far side of the Isle of Wight before two torpedoes struck amidships.

The ship went down almost immediately with the loss of most of her crew of 850 men.

The first the Turner family knew about the tragedy was when a boy cycled up to the house with a telegram. Mrs Turner tore it open with trembling hands and read the block letters. The message was brief.

HMS BARNABUS CAME UNDER ENEMY ATTACK AT 0200 HOURS ON 19 JANUARY STOP SHE SANK WITH THE LOSS OF MANY HANDS STOP ABLE SEAMAN WILLIAM TURNER IS MISSING PRESUMED DEAD STOP

Three months later a letter arrived from the king. Mrs Turner had it framed and hung above her bed, beneath a photo of her husband in naval uniform. King George said how sorry he was for her loss: her husband had died valiantly in the service of King and Country.

Her public grief was short. So many people were receiving bad news it seemed obscene to dwell on one's personal loss. When the war was over and done with, she could sort things out and mourn properly, decently, privately.

Then, out of the blue, the Turners had a visit from a stranger in uniform. He introduced himself as Petty Officer Fred Wareham, 'Bill's best mate'; he apologized for being 'one of the lucky ones'.

'Bill and I had a pact, see,' he explained in a lilting Welsh accent. 'If one of us went for a Burton and the other didn't, the survivor was to call on his mate's family . . . So here I am to tell you how much Bill loved you all.'

Mrs Turner dabbed her eyes with her sleeve. In a faltering voice, she said, 'Please come in, mister. It's kind of you to come.'

When the sailor was sitting in their front room alongside the aspidistra plant, Mrs Turner went to make a cup of tea, leaving him to tell the children about the war. As she returned with two cups of tea, she took the children to one side.

'Iris, be a good girl. Look after Tom for half an hour or so. I want to hear about your dad; I'll tell you later.'

Once she and the visitor were sitting either side of the big green plant, a cup of tea in their hands, she looked him in the eye and said, 'Let me have it straight, please. No frills.'

Fred's first words almost knocked her off her seat.

'Now I don't want to raise false hopes, missus, but there's a chance Bill's still alive. All I can tell you is what I saw with my own eyes, straight up, from start to finish.'

As Mrs Turner sat there, butterflies fluttering in her stomach, Fred told his story.

'Funny thing, the sea was so calm. We'd just passed the Needles, a bright moon lit up the waves like an oil painting. Lovely and still it was. I was on watch in the bow, Bill was lookout in the stern.

'All at once, I see these two light green shafts racing towards us at a rate of knots. Right away I realized what they were. I knew they'd sink us. The terrible thing was, there was nothing I could do—just stand and wait for the explosion.

'I hardly had time to shout a warning when I heard two dull thuds, like someone thumping on the door. They took us just below the waterline, so we had no chance.

'All was deathly quiet: the lull before the storm.

'Then, before I could draw breath, the whole ship shuddered from bow to stern as if her back was broken. After that she started to break up. The air was thick with choking black fumes and blood red flames. I felt her heaving as if she was about to spew; then followed a God Almighty explosion that split the ship in two.

'Our ship's alarm was roaring like a wounded bull. The captain was bellowing "ACTION STATIONS! ACTION STATIONS!" over the tannoy.

'But it was too late. We'd bought it.

'The next command from the skipper was "ABANDON SHIP! ABANDON SHIP!"

'All hell broke loose. It was every man for himself. Not that we had a choice. Sailors were rushing for lifeboats. Others were stumbling about in the smoke, desperately trying to escape the flames; those caught in the searing heat were screaming in pain and panic. Down below we could hear muffled explosions and cries from hands unable to climb the gangways.

'Worst of all were the silent ones, those engulfed in giant oranges of fire. I watched in horror as their twisted mouths uttered screams that were immediately swallowed up by the flames. Some flung themselves overboard and disappeared into the sea with an angry hiss.

'Real ghastly, it was!

'The ship first listed to port, then it keeled over and

sank within minutes. Most of the crew went down with the ship, trapped in their sunken tomb. They didn't have an earthly.

'By rights I should have joined them. But some of us got lucky and were blown into the sea. That's fate, isn't it? My guardian angel must have been looking down.

'The blast went and tossed me into the water alongside an empty oildrum, and I clung on for grim life in the freezing sea.

'I wasn't the only one. There were others struggling in the briny, and since Bill and I were on watch together, by my reckoning he could have been one of the survivors. Those in their bunks below hadn't a chance.

'Anyway, next thing I know there's this Jerry sub that had surfaced—a black sinister silhouette against the sky. Sailors were hauling our lads out of the drink and taking them down below. I guess our shipmates got whisked off to forced labour in Jerryland.

'There was one sailor—I couldn't make out his face; but I distinctly saw a tattoo on the back of his hand, between thumb and forefinger. The tattoo of a bird.

'Bill had one exactly like that; a dove, I think.

'Jerry couldn't have spotted me behind my oildrum, and I was dead scared of shouting in case I got a bellyful of salt water. I must have conked out shortly after, for the next thing I know I'm being winched aboard a rescue ship—one of ours—and brought back to Blighty. A blooming miracle, if you ask me.'

Realizing what little comfort that was for Mrs Turner, he added bitterly, 'I'll make the buggers pay!'

With a sigh, the sailor got up to go. It had not been an easy visit.

'Well, I've said my piece,' he said, putting on his cap. 'As I said, I don't want to raise false hopes, Mrs Turner. I wish you and the kids well whatever happens.'

She showed him to the door, shook hands limply and murmured after him, 'Thanks.'

Later that day, she sat the children down and told them the visitor's story, leaving out the gruesome bits.

'It's just possible, children, that your dad was rescued by a German ship and is now a prisoner-of-war,' she said, wiping her eyes.

'Does that mean we might see Dad come home one day?' asked Tom.

'Maybe,' said Mrs Turner. 'When this war's all over.'

That gave them all hope.

'I wish I was old enough to kill Germans,' was all Iris said.

Tom kept silent.

6

Searching for Wreckage

The morning after the plane crash was crisp and cloudy. As it was Sunday, Tom and Iris were at a loose end. Normally, they'd be at Sunday School across the road. But what with glass and rubble strewn about, Jesus would have to wait. Prayers and hymns were cancelled for the time being.

The Revd Nigel Pattison didn't fancy holding an open-air service with bombs dropping on his head.

He had posted up a notice on the still upright oak door of the church:

CHURCH SERVICES CANCELLED
GOD IS ON OUR SIDE
ONLY THE DEVIL BOMBS CHURCHES

Someone had added in pencil, 'Suffer little children to come unto me.'

Iris was disappointed. She looked forward to Sunday School with its lantern slides of the Good Shepherd and Good Samaritan; she loved the children's hymns— 'Jesus Wants Me for a Sunbeam' and 'I'm H-A-P-P-Y, I'm H-A-P-P-Y. I know I am, I'm sure I am, I'm H-A-P-P-Y'.

They made her feel happy even when she wasn't. For a couple of hours inside this dream palace she could forget the war, her missing dad, the Brickwoods, and all that.

The songs would soar up to the high vaulted ceiling of the great church, echo round the rafters and bounce back down about her ears. You only had to cough and Jesus would hear you at the other end of the nave. She would walk down the aisle to the church hall where the children gathered, her shoes click-clacking through the

21

huge space and she would gaze up at the stained-glass windows that looked so magnificent and beautiful with the sun streaming through.

Iris hardly dared glance at the white stone altar with its purple cover and pure white damask cloth—out of bounds to all but the blessed, divided by a line separating Heaven and Earth, saints and sinners.

Now the palace walls were breached, the stained-glass windows smashed, the blessed altar reduced to rubble.

'Onward Christian soldiers, marching as to war . . . '

What were they to do on boring old Sunday, now that the church was bombed? Mum hated the kids under her feet while she was cooking Sunday dinner and doing the week's washing in the copper. Gran usually popped in for a natter, while Gramps pottered about, mending bits and pieces and talking to the cats. It was best to make yourself scarce on Sunday mornings.

Iris had a brainwave.

What about going in search of war souvenirs? Tom wouldn't need much persuading. Truth to tell, it was their favourite pastime. Both of them had a box of treasure. Iris's collection boasted six spent cartridge cases, three bullets (two of which she'd bought for a penny each off a boy at school) and . . . a jagged grey strip of metal with the marking HE 219A on it. She knew HE stood for Heinkel; so the metal must have fallen from a German plane.

She had stumbled upon it in a cabbage allotment while out picking rabbit food.

That wasn't her prize possession though. The jewel in her crown was a ten mark note with Adolf Hitler's face and a swastika on it. Grandad had presented it to her; he had swapped a packet of Woodbines for it at the prisoner-of-war camp over the hill at Southwick.

One Sunday morning after church, Grandad had told her and Tom about the German prisoners, mostly shot-down pilots and gunners. They could sometimes be seen in parks and gardens in their brown denims and peaked forage caps.

'Some are decent sorts, farm boys who'd sooner be digging up turnips and mucking out cows than fighting a war. They were forced into soldiering, and most of them have no time for old Adolf.'

A steely glint would come into Grandad's watery eyes.

'Some of them, though,' he continued in a low tone, 'would stick a knife in your back as soon as look at you. You can see the hate in their eyes.'

It was somehow odd to think of Germans as 'decent sorts'. Grandad must be going soft in his old age. What did he know about this war? Still, Iris was grateful for the German money. It was the envy of her schoolchums, not to mention her brother.

All Tom had in his collection was a couple of rusty cartridges smelling of gunpowder. He longed to add to it and make The Big Find one day. Both he and Iris dreamed of grander trophies. Maybe a Luger pistol or a pair of pilot's goggles.

Now was their chance.

'Why don't we go hunting for wreckage?' Iris suggested.

'What wreckage?' asked Tom suspiciously. 'Not your musty old bombed houses again!'

'Last night's plane, stupid!' she exclaimed, eyes raised to the heavens. 'We know it came down somewhere near the clay pits. Maybe the Home Guard won't have found it yet.'

Tom's eyes lit up.

'Crumbs!' was all he said. 'We might find something really fantastic. You know, an enemy gun or Iron Cross or something.'

'Or you might go and drown yourselves in those pits!'

It was Mum's cross voice from the kitchen.

'Just you keep away from them or you'll feel my hand round your ear. D'you hear me? They're treacherous.'

23

The old clay pits were the favourite haunt of local kids. Down the years workmen had scooped out spadefuls of clay from the area, and rain had filled the holes, so that they now formed five or six big ponds. Gradually, nature had taken its course and stocked them with pondlife: reeds and plants, frogs and newts, sticklebacks and bloodsuckers.

But today the children's quest was not frogspawn. It was a far more exciting catch: a German bomber!

To reach the pits they had to cross the railway line by Hilsea Halt. They trod warily, listening out for the whistle and chooff-chooff-chooff of an oncoming steam engine.

Once safely over the rails, they pushed a way through briar and bramble into a wooded copse. And as the trees thinned out, they glimpsed water glittering in the sunshine.

'What do we do if a German jumps out on us?' whispered Tom to his sister.

'Don't be daft,' she replied in a hoarse half-whisper. 'You saw him go down. His brains'll be down in his boots after the crash. I shouldn't think there's anything left of him—just toenails and mashed bones.'

'But you said you saw a parachute,' persisted Tom.

'Nah, more likely a wisp of white smoke or puff of shell fire.'

She didn't quite believe that herself. But it was big sister's duty to stop little brother worrying himself to bits.

'Anyway,' she continued, 'soldiers will have recovered the bodies by now or taken pilot and gunner prisoner. They can hardly swim all the way home across the Channel. So they'd have to turn themselves in, wouldn't they?'

The children were in for a shock.

7

Finding the Plane

As Iris and Tom emerged from the trees, they slithered down the muddy bank of the nearest pit, holding on to whatever clump of grass they could. Once beside the pond, they scanned the water for signs of wreckage. But the cloudy, slimy surface betrayed no clues.

'It's not deep enough to hide a plane,' said Iris. 'In the middle maybe, but bits'd be floating about, wouldn't they?'

She was feeling cheated at the thought of the plane sinking without trace.

They explored each of the other water holes. No luck. All they saw were the usual water creatures. Now that they weren't looking for them, the water teemed with newts and frogs and sticklebacks.

'You'd think they'd gathered on purpose, poking their tongues out at us,' said Tom in disgust.

He sent a stone skimming across the surface of the pond.

'Well, that's that,' he said in some relief. 'Let's get back.'

The eerie quiet was starting to bug him.

They retraced their steps towards the trees. Iris decided to take the long way home—just in case they came upon something—through the wood to the north of the railway line.

Most people steered clear of this neck of the woods. Its gnarled oaks and elms grew so densely that you could barely glimpse the sky even through the thinning branches of autumn.

But there was another good reason why decent folk avoided the wood: it was reputed to be haunted. Before the war a man walking his dog had come upon a woman's arm poking out of a shallow grave. The police had neither caught the murderer, nor traced the victim's identity. Rumour had it that they were German spies and the murder had been hushed up.

Now, in late September, the whiff of woody decay filled the air and the squelchy carpet of leaves gave off a heady malty smell.

Yet, all of a sudden, the children caught something else in the woods. They both lifted their heads together and sniffed the air, trying to place it.

'What's that pong?' asked Tom, wrinkling his nose.

'Poooh! Smells like burnt rubber or spent fireworks,' said Iris, pinching her nose. 'Strange: it's a bit early for Guy Fawkes.'

They stared at one another. Perhaps . . . It was slowly dawning on them what the smell could mean. Nervously they edged through the trees in silence, guided by the stench and the gritty ash in nose and mouth. It was not long before they found what they were looking for.

A patch of grey-blue sky suddenly widened above a clearing. Twisted tree trunks reeled back, stripped of leafy cover. Snapped branches poked spindly white fingerbones at the open sky; and freshly-dug brown earth lay upturned as if a legion of moles had been at work.

There before them, its nose buried deep in the dark soil, was an aeroplane. It was smaller than they expected. Perhaps that was because it was part buried in the earth, and the tail section and one wing had broken off.

The missing wing was caught in the brawny arms of an ancient yew tree—small wonder these trees were known as 'guardians of the dead'.

The mangled tail lay in a black pool of mud and brackish water some distance from its body.

Tom let out a scream of horror. He couldn't help it.

He was terrified more by the stark black cross on the grey fuselage and the hated swastika on the broken tail than by the burnt-out wreckage.

Iris was scared too. But she tried to put a brave face on it. After all, it had been her idea to search for the crashed plane. And now that they'd found it, they had to overcome their fear and take their just reward; they'd earned it.

She squeezed her brother's hand.

'It's OK, it's OK, Tommy,' she said in hushed tones. 'A crashed plane can't hurt you. Come on, let's take a look. Maybe we'll find those goggles you've always wanted.'

But Tom was rooted to the spot.

'C-c-can you s-s-see any dead bodies?' he stuttered.

Iris plucked up courage and stepped warily towards the main body of the plane. She had to hold a hanky to her nose: even now patches of fuel were smouldering all around and filling the air with an acrid stench.

If she stood on tiptoe, she could just peer into the cockpit through the cracked perspex window. All she could make out was a charred mass; it could be anything. If there was a dead body in there, it was unrecognizable.

'He's had his chips,' was all she said. 'Come on, let's take a dekko at the tail.'

Iris was several paces ahead of her brother; his attention was drawn to what looked like a black wallet in a clump of ferns. As he bent down to examine the unexpected find, Iris moved on. She was tramping down the undergrowth, making for the tail.

She had almost reached the wreck when she saw it . . .

In the nick of time she plugged her mouth with one fist to stifle a scream!

What at first she believed to be a woodland pool wasn't water at all. It was dark red liquid that had oozed out from beneath the tail fin, forming one large pool with several tributaries that meandered off through nettle beds, celandine, and bracken. The smell was vile.

An allied army of ants, bluebottles, and horseflies was feeding off this tasty meal.

Iris took control of herself, glanced anxiously towards Tom and, seeing him absorbed with his treasure, leaned against the tail. She felt sick. Morbid curiosity, however, drew her gaze to the other side of the wreck. She wished she hadn't looked.

She saw no body. Just bits of what was once a human being: an arm stump, splintered bones, staring eyes. 'Death sustains life in the forest,' she had read somewhere.

Tom's voice rescued her from the hideous scene.

'Found anything?'

She wanted to give a hasty no, but just a squeak squeezed from her throat. Turning away, she stumbled towards her brother, as white as a sheet, slumping on to a fallen tree trunk.

In his excitement, Tom did not notice his sister had turned a putty colour.

'Golly, see what I've found!' he cried. 'It's a German wallet—with photos and foreign words. Look.'

He handed her a black and white family snapshot, showing an older man and woman standing behind a little girl and a boy of about fourteen.

'Mmmm, she's nice,' said Tom, staring at another photo, this time of a girl. 'It's got her name on the back—see.'

Iris took it from him and read the words '*Mein Liebling*' on the back of the photo.

'Funny name for a girl,' muttered Tom.

He took back the photos, afraid that Iris might swipe his prize. Quickly, he stuffed the wallet into his jacket pocket.

'Just wait till I show them at school!' he exclaimed, eyes shining.

'Let's get out of here,' was all Iris said.

Tom was starting to feel queasy himself. The whole petrol-soaked glade could catch fire at any moment. As Iris went to grab Tom's arm to pull him away, however, they both froze in terror.

From the dark wood came a muffled groan. It was a most terrible, unearthly sound.

They both felt as if a cold, clammy hand had seized them by the scruff of the neck.

There. It came again.

'OOOOO-ooooo-hhh! OHHH-hhh-OHHH!'

8

The German Pilot

'What was that?' squeaked Tom.

Iris just wanted to grab him and run like the clappers. But she forced herself to stay cool, even though her heart was racing like an express train and she was quaking in her boots. Whatever happened, she had to keep Tom calm.

'Don't panic! Don't panic!' she told herself.

It couldn't be the Ghost of Haunted Wood. She didn't believe in all that mumbo-jumbo. She was past trusting in fairies, hobgoblins, Father Christmas, evil spirits; she even had her doubts about God after all the wickedness of the war. Surely the Devil couldn't be blamed for everything?

War soon put paid to childhood faith.

Someone was in pain, wounded, maybe dying.

She had picked up some First Aid in the Brownies; and here was a chance to put it to good use, to be a real Florence Nightingale.

Tom meanwhile was shivering with fright.

'Stay put and don't move,' she ordered in a commanding voice. 'I'll go and take a quick look-see.'

But Tom wouldn't leave her side.

So, like Hansel and Gretel, brother and sister advanced slowly, hand in hand, one step at a time. They moved towards the dense, dark trees. But it wasn't a house of gingerbread and barley sugar that stood before them.

It was a giant mushroom. The mushroom's white canopy had got tangled in the treetops, so that its load was now swinging to and fro, pendulum-like, head-high above the forest floor.

Here was their ghost. He was dressed in navy blue overalls, and had long brown boots and a grey leather flying helmet on his head. His eyes were closed, and strands of fair hair were stuck to his brow. Blood had dried beneath his nose and ears, and at the corners of his mouth.

'Is he . . . is he dead?' asked Tom, so quietly she could barely hear.

'Not as long as he's groaning,' she said with a wry smile. 'Dead men don't groan. Mind you, if we leave him here much longer, he'll most likely choke on his own blood.'

'We've got to do something,' whispered Tom. 'We can't just leave him to die. It'll take hours to fetch help.'

Iris gave her brother a grumpy look.

'Whose side are you on?' she said crossly. 'Why should we help a German? We didn't ask him to bomb us!'

She couldn't understand her brother, not after what had happened to Dad. If Mum were here she'd surely claw out the man's eyes.

Tom was stubborn.

'But the Germans helped Dad when they took him prisoner,' he argued. 'It wouldn't be fair if we let him die, would it?'

Iris ignored him: she was thinking.

'I suppose he might have secrets,' she murmured, half to herself. 'Soldiers could winkle them out of him.'

She made up her mind.

'Grab his legs while I try to unhook the 'chute.'

It was easier said than done. At first they attempted to pull him free, yanking and tugging the pilot's legs and arms—first one way, then the other. But that only tightened the noose around his neck.

'Go easy,' yelled Tom. 'You're strangling the poor devil.'

'He deserves to hang,' she grunted.

After a pause, she relented.

'Oh, hold on. I suppose I'll have to risk my neck.'

Hitching up her skirt and tucking it into her knickers, she reached up and swung herself into the tree which held the harness. She stuck first one foot in a cleft, then the other until she had climbed up to the branch supporting the harness.

She crawled along the branch, her feet and thighs gripping the tree, grazing knees and elbows in the process. Then she set to unravelling the parachute. It was slow, painstaking work, rather like trying to unknot a tangled fishing line. At last she called down, her words coming in puffs and pants:

'Hold on . . . tight . . . to his . . . f-feet.'

She unhooked one last cord and, with a tearing crash, the body slumped to the ground, knocking Tom over and half smothering him. At least he broke the fall.

As for Iris, the branch sprang sharply upwards, tipping her over and leaving her dangling in the air, several feet above the earth. She was left holding on by her toes and one hand.

There was nothing for it but to drop and hope for the best. With a despairing 'Here I come!' she went sprawling in a heap. At once she felt a sharp pain in her right ankle. But she didn't think it was broken.

'Ouch!' she yelled. 'I almost ended up killing myself to save his miserable skin!'

Painfully, she picked herself up and stepped gingerly towards Tom. She pulled her brother free from under the body before turning her attention to the unconscious German. Together they laid him gently on his back upon the leafy soil.

He was still breathing, though his breath was coming in short gasps. He looked half dead already.

9

First Aid

Brother and sister gazed down at the body with a
mixture of fear and loathing. They had never set eyes on
a German before.

This was the enemy.

A fiend who'd murder them in their beds.

A monster who'd slit the throats of little children.

A Nazi who'd sunk their father's ship.

Iris felt more like kicking than helping him. But she
needed to keep him alive for the soldiers. And if she
didn't help him breathe, he'd soon choke to death. So
she gave a sharp order to Tom.

'Go and find a tin can. Fill it with water from the
nearest pit and bring it here. Fast!'

While Tom dashed off, she took out her white
handkerchief and moistened it on her tongue. With
one hand holding up the man's head, she first rubbed off
the caked blood from under his nose and mouth. Then,
having undone the helmet strap, she wiped the sweat off
his forehead and brushed twigs and leaves from his hair.
He had a bad gash behind one ear, which started
bleeding as soon as she had cleaned it.

She tore a strip off the bottom of her blouse and used
it as a bandage round his head, tying a knot at the
opposite side to the wound. There. Pity about the
blouse.

With fair hair tumbling over his brow, he looked so
calm and peaceful now that he was cleaned up. She was
surprised how young he looked, almost a boy—only a
few years older than herself. She gazed down at him and
gave a timid smile.

Funny how you always picture Germans as ugly,

vicious, and cruel, she thought to herself, as they do in the *Beano* and *Dandy*. Yet he looks so harmless, quite handsome too.

Then she shook her head, as if clearing it of unwanted thoughts.

What am I thinking of? There's no reason why *all* thugs should look ugly and evil. Evil is what evil does!

She'd read that somewhere or other. How true it was.

When Tom returned with a tinful of muddy water, she washed off the remaining blood, sweat, and dirt.

'That'll do,' she said, turning to a badly twisted arm. 'It looks broken just below the elbow.'

As her fingers groped for the break, digging into the flesh of the bad arm, the pilot's face creased with pain. He moaned softly and his eyes flickered open.

'Oh, my God!' gasped Tom, starting up. 'He's going to do us in.'

But the German was in no fit state to move, let alone do them harm. His dull grey eyes stared fearfully at the children, trying to take in the situation.

They were enemies, even if they were children. He was in hostile hands. Were they out to kill or help him? He found it hard to focus his eyes and his mind. He felt so tired that at that moment he didn't really care what happened to him.

Iris wasn't sure what to do. If they ran for assistance, he might escape or even die . . . While she was making up her mind, a gurgle came from his throat. His whole body trembled from top to toe and he lifted the good hand towards his mouth.

'*Wasser!*' he murmured.

'I think he wants a drink,' said Tom.

'He's welcome,' she muttered. 'As long as he doesn't mind a tadpole or two.'

As Iris held up his head again, Tom put the tin can to the man's lips, spilling most of the water down his chin. The wounded pilot swallowed the dirty water greedily.

It seemed to revive him a bit, for he spoke again, this time with a pained smile of thanks.

'*Danke.*'

With that he closed his eyes and sank back on the damp earth. His teeth were chattering and beads of sweat were breaking out on his brow like raindrops on a window pane.

'Can't we get him to somewhere warm?' asked Tom, appealing to his sister.

Iris had been thinking of that herself. Not that she wished to improve his lot. Her first thought was to stop him escaping before they had interrogated him.

He was *their* prisoner, *their* responsibility, *their* contribution to the war.

Though she didn't mention it to Tom, there was something else on her mind, something hard to put into words. If she didn't try to save his life, as the Germans *might* have done for Dad, that would make her worse than them . . .

She had to show that the British, at least, were *civilized*. They were fighting a war only in self defence.

10

'My Name is Martin'

Iris came to a decision.

'Right, let's take him to the old railway shed. We can lock him in there while we go for help.'

'He'd be warmer too,' added Tom.

Beside the railway line, about a hundred yards south of the Halt, stood an abandoned railway shack. Once upon a time it had been used by workmen for storing their tools; but it had lain empty for as long as the children could remember. Last year they'd used it as their secret den.

As brother and sister were talking, a chill breeze had sprung up and the first drops of rain were falling from an iron-grey sky.

'I'd better patch up his arm,' said Iris, taking off her woolly scarf.

She made a makeshift sling from her brown scarf and, as gently as possible, tied it round neck and forearm. The sharp pain as she lifted the arm roused him once more. By now he understood that the children were trying to help. So, when they made signs for him to stand up, he did his best to obey.

With his good arm leaning on Iris's shoulder, and with Tom propping him up from behind, the airman painfully rose to his feet. Resting on the children, he stepped forward, stumbled, recovered and took one short pace at a time.

It was slow going, especially with Iris limping on her sprained ankle. Yet after half an hour they made it to the old wooden shed beside the track.

'Lift the wooden bar from the door,' Iris told her brother. 'I'll hold him up. Get a move on.'

After much effort, Tom lifted the heavy block and swung open the creaking door. It was dark and musty inside, full of cobwebs hanging from the corners in matted nests, and of rat droppings on the floor.

The walk seemed to have done the prisoner good: he was now back among the living and realized that this was to be his prison cell. Bowing his head, he passed through the door unaided and collapsed on the floor in one corner.

'OK, Fritz,' said Iris in a firm voice. 'You—our prisoner. We go for police. You no escape. Savvy?'

She gave him a hard stare, just as her teacher did with her when she was chattering in class. The young man evidently understood the word 'police', for he nodded wearily.

'My name is Martin,' he said, holding out his good hand.

Perhaps he didn't like the name Fritz.

Tom shook his hand limply.

'I'm Tom, she's Iris,' he said.

'Oh, for Heaven's sake, Tommy,' said his sister crossly. 'We don't shake hands with Germans! They're—'

She stopped in mid-sentence, realizing what he had said. He had spoken English. Good English too. Was he a spy trained to eavesdrop on the enemy?

'CARELESS TALK COSTS LIVES'
'WATCH OUT, THERE'S A SPY ABOUT!'
'KEEP IT UNDER YOUR HAT!'

She remembered the warning posters.

But what on earth could he learn from them?

'Oh, so you speak English, do you?' she said roughly. 'All the better for getting secrets out of you.'

He smiled wanly.

'I have no secrets,' he said. 'Even if I had, I wouldn't betray my country. Would you?'

Iris frowned. She'd leave such moral issues to grown-

37

ups. Changing the subject, she said, 'Where did you learn English? Are you a spy?'

Martin sighed.

'My parents sent me to my English auntie in the school holidays before the war. I'm from Hamburg; the port did a lot of trade with England. And a few kids spent their vacation with English families.'

He smiled to himself as he recalled the happy times he had had in England.

'I stayed with my auntie's family in Winchester, not far from here—you know, where King Alfred burned the buns.'

'Cakes,' Tom corrected him. 'He burned the cakes.'

'Ah yes, cakes,' repeated Martin. 'Did you know Alfred was a Saxon, from Germany?'

Iris snorted.

'King Alfred was *English*! He was *our* king!'

Martin seemed to enjoy the joke. 'But the English were from Germany too—they were the Engels, a German tribe. You see, you and I are from the same stock.'

The history lesson had gone far enough. He was their prisoner, *not* their teacher; it was time to put him in his place.

'You Germans think you're so clever, don't you!' said Iris testily. 'You want to rule the world! Well, you won't. Never! We British will stop you.'

Martin was about to say something; but he thought better of it as Iris got ready to go.

She pulled Tom roughly through the door, eager to get away from the cocksure German. Slamming the door shut, she slotted the wooden bar into place. Then, taking Tom's arm, as much for support as for the need to hurry, she limped across the railway line.

Fate was unkind that day.

Just as they reached the other side of the rails, the dreaded siren wailed. The two children halted in their tracks.

'Oh no, not in broad daylight,' groaned Iris. 'On a Sunday too! No respect, the heathens!'

If she'd been fit and on her own, she might have risked it. But Tom was her responsibility, as Mum frequently reminded her. They needed to take shelter. And fast. Air raid warnings only gave you a few minutes.

It was either the trees or the shed. However ghastly the thought of sheltering with a German, there really wasn't much choice.

'Back to the shed,' she yelled.

The prisoner must have expected the police. For as they threw open the door he was standing there, one hand high in the air, the other helpless in a sling.

'Bombs!' was all Iris said. '*Your* bombs!'

He'd heard the siren. In any case, the disgust on the girl's face made everything clear.

'I'm sorry,' he said.

11

Rain

The shed had no benches, not even a wooden box to sit on. The only sign of one-time human use was a pot-bellied black stove squatting in one corner like a smug Buddha. Its rusty iron doors were hanging off their bolts and rats had made nests where once a fire had blazed.

It was cold and damp inside the place and it stank to high heaven. But at least it kept out the rain and gave them a reassuring sense of security, as if flying shrapnel or bombs couldn't touch them.

Although the shed had no windows, they could let in fresh air and light by flinging the door open. The opening also gave them a bird's eye view of the town, since that section of railway track was on an incline.

All three had to sit or lie on the floor. And since Martin had bagged the far corner opposite the stove, the choice for the children was to sit either by the door or against the wall between stove and prisoner.

Neither fancied getting drenched by driving rain or splattered by shells, so they had to squeeze in beside the wounded German.

All three sat in silence, listening to the rain pattering on the roof, the wind howling in the trees, and the yew branches swishing high above them. Now and then, the harsh cawing of a crow made them jump—it was so like someone crying out in pain.

The shrieking crow must have reminded Martin of something because he suddenly broke the silence.

'Excuse me. Did you find anything—besides me, I mean?'

'We found your plane,' said Tom before Iris could stop him.

Martin's eyes shone hopefully.

'Ah, so . . . Anything else?'

Iris kept quiet. Tom looked guiltily into space and bit his lip; his right hand involuntarily clutched the bulging jacket pocket.

Their reluctance to speak gnawed away at Martin's heart. Up till now, he had been lost in his own pain, drifting in and out of reality. Now, with his pain eased and his body cleaned up, his mind was able to focus on matters outside himself.

He and Erich, the tail gunner, had grown up together in Hamburg, on the banks of the Elbe. They had joined the same detachment of Hitler Young Folk; they had marched and sung in torchlight processions; they had shared hopes and fears and, sometimes, doubts together.

It was their staunch friendship that had helped them survive the terrible nightmare of the bombing of their homes. And when they joined the Luftwaffe, the commanding officer had let them form a pilot-gunner team.

This was their first big mission together, in a brand new Messerschmitt. How proud they had felt to be chosen to bomb enemy targets. Both dreamed of winning the Iron Cross.

More than that, they owed it to their loved ones to punish the English for their barbarity.

Martin had to know the truth. And Tom seemed the more likely source of information.

'Tom,' he said quietly, 'may I ask you a question, man to man? This is very painful for me. You see, my best friend was with me in the plane. Erich. Erich Kastner. Did you . . . ?'

Tom glanced at Iris and, seeing her warning glare, shook his head slowly. He was not a good liar, and Martin could tell by his red neck that he was holding something back. There was nothing for it but to appeal directly to this cold, hostile girl.

'Miss,' he began—he didn't dare use her name—'I know you don't like me. I can't blame you. If I'd found an English pilot who'd bailed out over Hamburg, I'd hate him like poison for all the death and destruction he'd caused.'

His words only incensed Iris even more. How dare he hate English airmen! It wasn't them who were evil; it was the Germans. She wanted to hurt him with the truth. There could be no harm in him knowing—he'd soon be in custody anyway.

'If you must know,' she said with a sneer, 'we found your plane—what was left of it. And your friend—what was left of him!'

Tom stared at her in horror. Was she telling the truth or trying to spite him? He watched the prisoner's face: his head slumped back against the cobwebbed wall, his eyes closed, his jaw bones were working as if chewing on a lump of coke, and tears squeezed through the corners of his screwed-up eyes.

Iris at once felt remorse for her callous outburst. Tom's accusing look didn't help. Death was death, whoever it was. And friends were friends, whoever they were.

She looked away. It was uncomfortable to see a man cry. Strange too: Germans were heartless, after all.

In the eerie quiet, broken only by raindrops pattering on the roof, the two children stared at the floor, not wishing to intrude further on his grief.

It was Tom who finally spoke.

For some time he had been fidgeting, as if the bare boards were boring into his bottom. His right hand kept fluttering from floor to pocket, unable to keep still. At last, his hand made up its mind. It dived into the side pocket of his grey flannel jacket and fished out The Great Find.

'I found this,' he blurted out.

Slowly, the grey watery eyes opened, trying to focus on the black object in the grubby hand. With his good fist Martin rubbed his eyes and gave an embarrassed cough to clear his throat.

'You can have it,' said Tom, 'in memory of your friend.'

Martin looked fondly at the trophy, coughed again, then muttered hoarsely, 'Thank you.'

Somehow Tom had to say something more, anything to dispel the suffocating atmosphere of the shed, to heal the wound his sister had opened.

'I hope you don't mind. I looked inside. Two photos . . . Was that his family? Girlfriend? Her name's on the back—Mina or something.'

For a few moments Martin didn't answer. His eyes had closed and his head had dropped forward, lost in painful memories. At last he looked up and gazed at Tom; the boy deserved an answer.

'No, I don't mind. I'd have done the same. I used to collect war souvenirs myself back home. My prized possession was a packet of Craven A cigarettes; it had a black cat on the box—must have fallen from a crashed RAF bomber.'

Martin hesitated, uncertain of his next words.

'The wallet . . . It isn't Erich's. It's mine.'

12

Interrogation

Tom was so surprised he held out the wallet to its rightful owner.

All the time Iris had held her tongue. Although she regretted losing her temper, she was becoming more and more uneasy at this fraternization with the enemy. It didn't seem right and proper. She needed to reassert her authority, make the captor–captive relationship crystal clear.

'I'll take that!' she snapped.

As if to explain herself, she added, 'I need to check it for documents and secret compartments.'

She snatched the wallet from Tom's hands and set to sifting through the worn leather pockets. She was to be disappointed. As she shook it over her lap, all that tumbled out were the two black and white snapshots, a brown stamp and three mark notes, all bearing Hitler's head, and what appeared to be an identity card.

Picking up the card, she studied the tiny photo above words and figures she couldn't make out. All she managed to decipher was the year '1926' and a name 'MARTIN POHL'.

She looked up sharply, glanced sternly from photo to prisoner—as if checking the likeness—and said in an adult voice, 'Presumably this is you. The police will be interested in that.'

She thrust the identity card into her skirt pocket. Martin sighed; he made no objection.

Iris was now in command, showing him who was boss.

After a long pause, she picked out the family snapshot from among the items on her lap and held it up. An unspoken query hung in the air.

'Yes,' Martin said grimly, 'that's my family. Or, rather, it was: mother, father, and sister Gretchen—they're all dead; my sister and mother were killed by *your* bombs.'

Iris ignored the last comment. The English bombed airfields, war factories, munitions plants—*not* families. No doubt the Nazis fed him this propaganda so as to make him desperate to fight. Her thoughts were interrupted by Martin.

He was pointing to the picture.

'That's me when I was about your age, four years ago. I was thirteen at the time.'

Tom was eager to break in. His sister's harsh tone upset him.

'So it *is* your wallet,' he said. 'I found it, you know.'

Martin appealed once more to the more sympathetic boy.

'May I have the pictures? You are welcome to the wallet and the rest.'

Tom looked at his sister hopefully. But she hadn't finished her interrogation.

'What's this second picture?' she asked suspiciously, turning it over to read the two words on the back—as if they were some secret code.

Martin frowned, bowed his head and said quietly, 'That is Erich's sister. She's—how do you say?—my girlfriend, my childhood sweetheart. I've known her since I was nine.'

'What do the words mean?' persisted Iris.

He smiled to himself: here was a little girl playing at grown-ups. Let her have her fun.

'*Mein Liebling*—that's German for My Sweetheart,' he said gravely.

Even Iris seemed embarrassed at forcing such personal matters into the open.

'Oh,' she said. 'Is that all?'

Without further ado, she put the two photos into his outstretched hand.

45

'She's nice,' said Tom.

'Thank you,' replied Martin to both children at once.

He looked lovingly at the creased picture and for a moment he was far, far away—back home, before raids, before bombs, before war.

'Her name's Anna,' he said fondly, coming back to the present. 'I'll tell you about her, if you like, and Erich and myself as kids.'

'Yes, please,' said Tom keenly.

Martin looked at the self-appointed Commandant.

Iris shrugged her shoulders and nodded curtly.

13

Martin's Story

You know, the trouble with you English is that you think all Germans are Nazis and adore Adolf Hitler. Not so. Take my family and Erich's. Although we were very close, our parents were forever squabbling over politics.

My family lived in an old grey-stone house alongside the church where Grandad was Pastor. When he was young, Grandad had been a missionary in India, so he spoke good English, though with a funny Indian accent. He loved English poetry—Byron, Shelley, Wordsworth, even Kipling whom he once met in India.

Dad was Grandad's assistant, what you call a curate; and Mum too helped out in church, cleaning, arranging flowers and hymn books, that sort of thing.

Erich's family lived nearby, down by the river. His dad worked in the shipyards, on submarines. He'd made his way up from shop floor to chief engineer. Mr Kastner was a regular churchgoer and our choirmaster. However, that didn't stop him from taking Grandad to task for not supporting Hitler in his sermons.

I recall vividly one set-to they had over Sunday dinner. I guess I was twelve at the time. Erich's family often joined us at table after the morning service. Anyway, as usual, Erich's father was singing Hitler's praises.

'Pastor, you ought to tell the congregation that God sent us our great Leader; surely he wouldn't have been able to sort out the mess Germany was in so quickly otherwise. Do you remember how things were before 1933? No work, not enough to eat, prices going through the roof. And Germany was nobody in the world, everyone spat on her.'

'The man's a lunatic,' Grandad snorted. 'There are none so blind as those who will not see . . . Don't *you* see that this madman is leading us to disaster? Hitler builds an army. Hitler occupies the Rhineland. Hitler makes himself army chief. Hitler takes Austria back into the Reich! What next, I wonder? The world?'

The choirmaster's face had turned red at this insult to his idol. But he fought to control himself in front of the families seated round the bare oak table.

In a gentler tone he continued, 'Who would have thought, five years ago, that a mere army corporal would lead our nation to such greatness? Hitler has given us light in our hour of darkness. What does he get out of his devotion? Not riches, not privileges. He doesn't smoke, he doesn't drink, he doesn't eat meat, he even does without a family.

'All for our sake. If only we were all as selfless as Adolf Hitler. He is a model Christian. For the first time in our history, Germans are banding together, they feel proud, they can hold their heads up in the world. That's why they love Hitler, they will follow him anywhere, they are loyal to him.'

'What choice have they got?' asked Grandad. 'You can only vote for one party; and if you disagree with Hitler . . . you get shot or dragged off to a camp. Yesterday the Communists, today the Jews, and tomorrow the Christians, anyone who dares speak up. Mark my words, the man is crazy! He'll get us all killed!'

Erich's father saw there was no reasoning with Grandad. Instead, he turned to the four children: Erich and me, my sister Gretchen and Erich's younger sister Anna.

'Children, I envy you. The future belongs to you young folk. All the effort and sacrifice we make today will bring you and your children true happiness. Yes, children, I'm so proud to be German at this moment in history.'

We remained silent. We didn't know whom to believe. Mum and Dad were on Grandad's side; that was why I hadn't joined the youth group. Erich had signed up when he was ten, and I envied him his smart brown shirt with its triangular neckerchief, polished leather belt and boots. Most of my school were either in the Young Folk or, for older children, the Hitler Youth.

One day at school, I remember, all the classes had to assemble in the playground. Someone had already drawn chalk squares on the ground where each class had to stand. Our teacher led us out single file, marching smartly to take up our positions.

They put all those in brown shirts in the front ranks, while those in grey, green, or blue jackets—about two or three in each group—stood at the back.

In my form, as luck would have it, I was the only one to ruin the brown picture. In my dark green corduroy jacket and grey flannel trousers, I stood out like a thistle in a ripened wheatfield!

Our teacher brought us to attention like a squad of cadets and strode up and down the rows, inspecting us for dirty boots or sloppy dress. Then he called our names and we shouted our replies: 'Sir!'

When all was ready, the headmaster made his entrance. He walked slowly across the yard to a roll of drums and fanfare of bugles from a band of Hitler Youth. Despite his attempt at a dignified appearance, he cut a comical figure, being short and fat, with ruddy face, bald head, and a pair of old-fashioned glasses on the end of his nose.

Today, he too was dressed in brown, though his buttoned jacket was too tight for his belly.

He mounted the three steps to the platform placed before our proud ranks; a row of fifteen or so brown-shirted masters stood at his back. After waiting for absolute silence, he launched into his speech.

'Fellow Germans, we are gathered here today to celebrate the glory of our Fatherland. The German nation is great again. And it will be yet greater! Our lost peoples are coming home to us: Austria, the Saar, Sudetenland—all stolen from us by the Treaty of Versailles—as you know from your history books.'

By this time, he had worked himself up into a lather, imitating the passion of a Hitler or a Goebbels. He ranted on and on; and the longer the speech lasted, the more the boys and even some teachers grew restless and started talking among themselves.

This enraged the head. For he suddenly jumped down from his pedestal and started prowling round the ranks of boy soldiers, shouting at anyone who stood out from the mass.

Stomping back to his platform which raised him above the tallest head, he continued his tirade.

'As your headmaster, I am insulted by the lack of gratitude some of you show to our dear Leader—to whom we owe everything. I will not be content until I see only brown shirts all about me, do you hear? Only brown shirts! Until every boy is in the Hitler Youth! Until all our beloved Leader's enemies are destroyed! *Sieg Heil!* Hail Victory!'

His voice had reached fever pitch; but now it quickly dropped down the scale to a low, menacing growl.

'Remember: who isn't with us is against us. They are our enemies, our Leader's enemies, our Fatherland's enemies.'

His gaze fixed on my class. The glasses on the end of his nose glinted in the sunshine as he stared from boy to boy, shirt to shirt. All at once, he flung out a stubby arm—it was pointing straight at me!

'Look at him,' he screamed. 'The black sheep, the Judas goat, the disgrace to his class, his school. That boy has no shame, no gratitude to our Leader, he cannot be trusted!

'I am ashamed when I see such traitors in our midst. I want an army of loyal, strong boys of honour in my school.

'He who is not with us is against us. *Sieg Heil!*'

He flung up a rigid arm in Nazi salute.

I felt ashamed. I bowed my head, my face was as red as a turkey cock's, my legs were like jelly. What made it worse was that the other boys were now shuffling away from me; soon I stood all alone in the back row.

In other forms, too, boys were isolating the misfits.

Having made his point, the headmaster waved an angry hand towards the drummers and buglers. After the ominous silence, the roll of drums sounded like the death knell for us odd ones out, us traitors to the Fatherland.

Then the whole school, those in uniform and those without, took up the song:

'A young nation rises, ready for war!
Comrades, lift your banners high!
Our time is nigh,
The time of young warriors.
Ahead, with tattered, war-torn banners,
March the dead heroes of our young nation.
Above us, our heroic fathers gone before!
O Germany, O Fatherland, here we come!'

My voice rang out louder than the rest.

I did not want to be a traitor. I loved our Leader, our nation, our people. Whatever my parents said, *I was going to join the Young Folk!*

14

The Jews

Iris could contain herself no longer.

'Call yourself a Christian?' she said angrily. 'Then how come you bomb churches? Our vicar says God's on our side—only the Devil would destroy the House of God!'

It slowly dawned on Martin that *his* bomb had landed on a church. True enough: he knew he'd missed his target when he pressed the bomb release button. But what with all the flak about, it was hard to be sure. What would Grandad have said? 'A most shameful, un-Christian act, my boy!'

'I didn't mean to,' he mumbled. 'Was anybody hurt?'

'We don't think so,' said Tom. 'But you made a mess of the church and smashed all our windows.'

Martin seemed relieved.

'It was my first bombing mission.'

'And your last,' exclaimed Iris. 'At least you can't smash up any more churches or murder innocent people!'

'Don't your pilots bomb churches and hospitals?' he asked.

'I don't know about that,' she snapped back. 'Not on purpose anyway.'

She searched her mind for something else to fling at him.

'What about the Jews?' she asked coldly. 'Why do you kill them?'

She saw from the pained expression on his face that her barb had struck home. He looked most uncomfortable. In truth, he had never understood Hitler's quarrel with the Jews; all those he'd known in Hamburg were decent, hard-working, family people who'd never harmed a soul.

'Look,' he said slowly, 'I don't claim to understand everything. Our leaders say that Jews and communists tried to ruin Germany. Maybe they did. But I never killed any Jews. On the contrary. I tried to help . . . '

His mind drifted back to his childhood. He murmured, half to himself, 'Maybe I didn't do enough.'

After a long pause, he spoke again, so quietly the rain almost drowned him out.

'There are some things you can't defend. I used to play football with a good friend, Jacob Baruch. After a match one day, he invited me home for a glass of tea. "I want you to meet someone," he said.

'I'd never been into the Jewish quarter of the city before, so I was curious to go. Of course, I'd heard plenty of tales about the Jews, especially at school from teachers and at camps from our youth leaders—though I took it all with a pinch of salt. My parents were always telling me Hitler needed a scapegoat for his policies.

'The first thing that struck me in the Jewish quarter were slogans painted on walls and shop windows.

' "DON'T BUY FROM JEWS!"

' "PIG JEWS!"

'And passers-by, hurrying on their way, heads bowed, all wore yellow stars on their coats. How odd.

'At the corner of Jacob's street stood a big beefy bloke, legs planted wide apart. He was wearing grey army trousers tucked into long leather boots, a yellow shirt, and red armband with a black swastika on his left sleeve. The thumb of his left hand was stuck behind the buckle of his belt.

'As I turned the corner with Jacob, he gave us both a hostile stare, thrusting out his lower jaw. But he said nothing and let us by. Jacob led the way into a shabby building and up the stairs.

'The Baruch flat was full to bursting with little children. There was a sad-eyed skinny lad huddled in the corner; I'd not seen him before. Despite the summer heat, he was shivering.

'"This is David," said Jacob. "He's my cousin; he escaped from Schwerin. Go on, tell him, David."

'Words tumbled from the skinny youth like coins from a fairground machine.

'"They came for us in the night . . . beat us with rifles, shot the old and sick, even little kids, took us to a football field on the edge of town; then they lined us up and opened fire.

'"Mum fell on top of me, covering me with her body. When it was dark I crawled out. Everyone was dead; it was horrible."

'He broke down and sobbed as Jacob's mother put one arm round him, handing me my tea with the other.

'I didn't understand.

'"Were you sheltering communists?" I asked. "Was it revenge for killing a Nazi? Why should they do that?"

'"Because we're Jews," said Mrs Baruch quietly.

'As I walked home, my head was full of unanswered questions. But all my doubts dissolved like summer hailstones later that evening.

'Shouts, groans, curses, and the noise of tramping feet came from the highway at the bottom of our front garden. As I rushed to the window, I saw an astonishing sight. Coming down the road was a pitiful column of ragged women, children, and old men. They were flanked by soldiers, bellowing and hitting stragglers with their rifle butts.

'For one ridiculous moment it reminded me of a crowd of rival football fans being escorted away after a match. But where were the young men? Fans weren't tiny tots in nighties, women with streaming hair, old men on crutches, trying to walk with dignity—and soldiers treating people like cattle. Football fans got far more respect.

'We turned out the lights so as not to be seen. The column was now passing our gate and, all at once, I heard someone call my name.

' "Martin, win for me!"

'I couldn't see him in the gloom, but I knew the voice. Win what? Football? A place in Heaven? I wasn't sure what he meant.

'I never saw Jacob again. And no one ever mentioned the Jews, even in my household. We just didn't talk about them.'

15

'Once Upon a Time...'

Martin's voice tailed off and he screwed up his eyes as a spasm of pain seized him. After a moment his teeth began to chatter and his body shook in some sort of fever. He was lying awkwardly in the corner, back resting against the wall, broken arm across his chest. Now and again, as he lapsed in and out of consciousness, he let out a long groan or called '*Mutti*' softly.

Tom stood up, took off his jacket and draped it over the front of the sick man.

'What d'you want to do that for?' objected his sister, glaring at both of them.

'He's sick,' said Tom firmly.

He didn't care what his sister thought or what the prisoner had done. The man needed care and attention. Tom sat down on the other side of the German.

They remained like that, legs outstretched, sitting on the floor, each absorbed in their own thoughts. Martin now appeared to be sleeping, his breath coming in quick shallow gasps.

The light was fading from a murky grey to a sooty gloom as evening set in. From the darkness of the shed, the children stared out at the rain-filled sky. No stars, no moon, no planes. Yet just when they thought the siren had been a false alarm, they caught the sinister drone of bombers.

They could be heard but not seen above the dark rainclouds.

'Dorniers!' declared Tom.

'Heinkels,' said Iris, as if to spite him.

Whatever they were there were a lot of them. Trouble

was they presented an invisible target for the ground gunners, but equally, the pilots themselves had no clear view of the town.

Flares fizzed down with the rain.

It wasn't long before the children saw smoke and fire rising above the rooftops; it was coming from the direction of the town centre and dockyard. In their anxiety, Tom and Iris did not notice Martin waking up; all their thoughts were concentrated on Mum's safety. Where was she? Where were all their friends and relatives?

The sleep seemed to have done Martin good, for his shivers had subsided and his face was no longer creased in pain.

'Thanks for the coat,' he said gratefully to Tom. 'You are very kind, a Good Samaritan. One day I'll tell my grandfather of your Christian act; he'll be proud of the little English boy.'

He smiled weakly to himself before speaking again.

'But your sister's right: they're Heinkel bombers, HE One Eleven, if I'm not mistaken, with an escort of Messerschmitt 109s by the sound of it. Looks like we're in for a big blitz tonight.'

Iris was not flattered by his support. She was far more concerned with the danger they were in, and she was starting to be really scared. Never before had she sat through a raid without Mum. In Mum's calming presence she always felt secure. Now, the growing racket, the sweeping searchlights, the gun flashes were all driving her round the bend.

Not only that. She was starving, she'd had nothing since a slice of bread and plum jam at breakfast. If it hadn't been for *his* bomb, she'd have gone to church, had her dinner, listened to hymns on the wireless, and been safe with Mum.

She'd swap this draughty old railway shed for their smelly backyard shelter any day.

And what if Adolf decided to gas them tonight of all nights—when they had no gas masks?

It was all *his* fault.

If she didn't have enough on her plate, her brother was snivelling like a puppy. Iris was near to tears herself.

What was to become of them?

All of a sudden, a quiet, calming voice pierced the gloom. It seemed to come from another world, a world that was cosy and familiar.

'Once upon a time there was a little boy called Hansel and his sister Gretel. They lived in a large wood with their mother and father who were very poor . . . '

It was Martin. He was doing his best to take their minds off the bombs.

When no protest came, he continued the story in a sing-song voice, made all the more magical by the flickering sky and eerie sounds from the woods.

'One day, their father took the children deep into the forest and left them there . . . '

Slowly but surely he drew the children to him as to a magnet. Tom stopped crying so as to hear the words better. Even Iris, though initially staring sullenly into the night, was being drawn into the web woven by the storyteller. She kept darting a furtive glance towards the dark figure in the corner, hanging on to his every word.

As one tale ended, he drew another from his mother's treasure chest of German stories: 'Rumpelstiltskin', 'Snow White', 'Rapunzel', 'The Musicians of Bremen'. By the time he got to 'The Golden Goose', he had the children tittering at the scene:

'Stupid had the Golden Goose tucked under his arm, with the three maids stuck fast. Then came a lanky parson in a long black cloak, a fat policeman, two red-faced farmers with rake and hoe, a cat, a dog, and a little pink pig, all tripping over each other's feet . . . '

All three, storyteller and audience, seemed to be

under a magic spell, transported to the realm of fairy tale where anything was possible.

For the first time Iris started to take an interest in Martin as a person rather than a prisoner.

When the stories came to an end, she asked in a matter-of-fact voice, 'What did *you* do when war broke out?'

She was eager not to break the spell.

Martin was surprised at the change. But he, too, was keen to preserve the new trust. So he quickly said, 'Well, at the start of the war my father got called up, together with Erich's father. They went off to the eastern front, Dad as chaplain to the regiment, Erich's father as officer in the Gestapo. Thankfully, Grandad was too old for the front. So he continued his church work and, of a night, served in the flak and searchlight batteries.

'You English kept him on his toes; we had raids at least twice a week for three long years. So we also had our air-raid shelters, mostly in the basements of flats, though Mum and Grandma used to take Gretchen and me to the public round tower—the Winkel, as we called it.

'In next to no time Hamburg was a city of mainly elderly people, women, and children. But we did have many thousands of foreigners—"Eastern Workers" from Russia and Poland, whom we treated like slaves—and many POWs from France, Belgium, and even England. Someone had to run the shipyards on the far bank of the Elbe.

'Grandad used to address his flak unit with the words, "Girls and Boys, Comrades and Gentlemen!"'

'Comrades were the Russians, Gentlemen the English.'

'Did you go to school?' asked Tom.

'In a way, yes. Like all teenagers, Erich and I had to serve in the searchlight batteries. We slept, ate and had lessons in our unit. Each day was a mixture of gun drill

and makeshift classes with our old schoolteachers—
those who were over conscription age.'

'It must have been fun!' said Tom, eyes shining.

Martin pulled a sour face.

'It wasn't a game of cowboys and Indians,' he said.
'But it was our duty in the Hitler Youth to defend our
homes and families; and we felt proud to do so.'

'Did you really think you'd win the war?' asked Iris.

Martin felt like insisting: 'We *will* win the war!' But
he wanted to be truthful, and he was no longer so sure.

'At first I thought it would be over and done with in a
year. With Hitler to lead us how could we fail? Yet the
war somehow dragged on and on. I'll never forget
hearing Herr Goebbels on the wireless; he was giving a
speech in Berlin's Sports Palace. His words inspired yet
scared me, I can hear them now:

' "The English say that Germany is almost finished.
Are we? Shall we fight to the end?" '

'With tens of thousands of others, I shouted "YES!" '

'When Goebbels promised total war, I was with him.
That was last February, just after the disaster of
Stalingrad when the Russians blocked our advance.

'Shortly afterwards, Erich and I heard that our fathers
had both died in that battle. In my heart of hearts, I
then began to wonder whether we would win the war.'

His next words came as a shock.

'If it hadn't been for your inhuman crimes, I might
have lost heart. But what your war criminals did was
unforgivable. It made us all determined to fight to the
end!'

16

Catastrophe

By the middle of '43, a lot of people were getting sick and tired of the war. We knew we'd got ourselves into a pickle; the war was going all wrong. It seemed a long time since the cheery days of glorious victory after glorious victory. Now, nothing but bad news after bad news was coming from the fronts.

Other German cities had been badly bombed. When would it be our turn? The people of Hamburg were becoming jittery. A few even dared to think of defeat, though they were too scared to say so in case the Gestapo heard:

WATCH OUT!

BUTTON YOUR LIP!

SAY NOTHING!

Every night we lived in dread that the bombers would come again—this time in large numbers.

Yet life went on. Anna and I would go for quiet walks, hand-in-hand, along the banks of the Elbe or through the rose gardens. At the weekend we sometimes went to Carl Hagenbeck's famous zoo to see the lions and monkeys. And then of an evening we often went to the Ufa-Palast, the biggest cinema in Germany. Do you know, it even had a stage for a whole orchestra which would disappear through the floor when the film came on?

I'll never forget the day before the Catastrophe. It's written in blood upon my mind.

Saturday 27th July.

For many it was the last day on earth.

My youth group was getting ready for a canoe race on the Alster; we were expecting sixty-five teams from all

over the country on the Sunday morning. And we had to
work flat out to be ready: marking and clearing the
course, patching up our canoes, polishing the silver
cups, and getting in last-minute practice. Erich and I
were in the lead canoe.

We prayed that the fine sunny weather would last.

'God give us sunshine for the regatta.'

We should have prayed for heavy rainclouds to cover
Hamburg like a shroud! Better still, for the city to be
whisked off to the heavenly clouds instead of being
despatched down to Hell's inferno.

That evening I had to report back to my searchlight
battery at nine sharp. Just as well I did, for the sirens
sounded at twenty past nine. Only ten minutes later the
All-Clear followed. False alarm—as usual!

It was such a lovely summer night. The stars
glittered, the horse-chestnut smelt sweet, the man in
the moon smiled down on us all. Yet if you took a closer
look you could see sorrow in his smile that night. He
must have known what was to come.

Erich and I read and chatted until midnight. We had
both been taking flying lessons and were due to sit our
exams on the Monday. So we were busy testing each
other.

We were so excited about leaving the searchlight unit
and flying together. Somehow going on to the offensive
seemed more manly and useful than being in defence. It
was frustrating being stuck in a bunker, waiting for
enemy planes. How much more exciting it would be to
take the war to the enemy and bomb the living daylights
out of him!

I must have dozed off around midnight, but I didn't
get much shut-eye. We were woken by our trusty old
Luftgefahr 30—the thirty minute phone call to warn us
that bombers were on their way. I glanced at my watch:
nineteen minutes past midnight. We staggered from our
beds as the loudspeaker boomed out:

'ACTION STATIONS! ACTION STATIONS!'

'What a waste of time!' Erich grumbled. 'Alerts, alerts, alerts and nothing ever happens. I need my beauty sleep for the canoe race.'

Yet then a second warning came: the *Luftgefahr 15*.

This time the loudspeaker told us the enemy was gathering in force at Brunsbüttel for an assault on the city. We were all searching the skies to the west where we could expect to see the first flak fire soon. And we waited for further information from the radar post.

We had a couple of youngsters who'd been with us only a few days, and they were getting panicky, asking all sorts of questions:

'Will our noses bleed when the guns start firing?'

'Will the noise burst our eardrums?'

We old sweats did our best to calm them.

'No,' we said. 'But hold on to your heads or they'll fall off!'

At precisely 12.33 a.m. the *Fliegeralarm*, our main public siren, went off. It made an awful din. Now we knew for sure we were in for a busy night.

Like most people in the city, we kept our wireless switched on, listening out for instructions. The first sign that something really big was in the offing was when all stations went off the air. Not even any music. Just a crackling silence.

Not long after, the silence was broken by a calm, deep voice, one we'd come to trust. It was our State Secretary, George Ahrens. Everyone called him 'Uncle Aspirin' because he soothed the nerves.

'Aircraft approaching Hamburg in large numbers. The first bombs will fall in several minutes. Take cover.'

First came RAF Pathfinders, marking out positions by dropping bright target indicators—like firework rockets shooting white blobs downwards. The whole of the neighbouring district glowed in a white light from the flares.

Then the first 'Christmas Trees'—the *Tannenbaum*, all lit up in lights and tinsel—began to fall. Almost at once came, one after the other, phosphorus, blast, and fire bombs—red, green, and gold. They floated down towards the ground like party balloons, popping into flowing strips that dropped on the houses, most of which were already in flames.

There were fires burning everywhere, even on the water and barges. I had never thought water could burn—I guess it was patches of oil spilling out of the boats. My first thought was of our boatshed with its precious canoes! They'd better not damage them! We were racing tomorrow!

Erich and I were operating our searchlight, groping in the dark, reaching out with ghostly yellow arms through the clear, starlit sky, trying to catch a moth for our gunners to shoot at.

What with the searchlights and the flares, it was as light as day, so light you could have read the daily *Tageblatt*.

The engine drone above us was getting louder and louder. Every gun, from onshore flak to ship's battery in the harbour, was blazing away with everything they had. In the heat of battle we seventeen-year-old *Spiddelfinken*—'skinny ragamuffins'—didn't even notice that we were shining our searchlights in completely the wrong direction. It wasn't really our fault. The master radar searchlight seemed to have gone haywire. Planes normally showed on the green radar screen as a small spike; but now the whole screen was covered in spikes as in a hailstorm. What on earth was happening?

Only afterwards did we learn that the enemy had 'spiked' our screens by dropping tons of aluminium strips. So it was a bit like going around in a dark room with a torch, trying to find a fly. Our flak defences just had to fire away blindly into that patch of sky where they hoped the bombers were.

The moment the golden rain had begun to fall, we could see people scurrying through the streets to the public shelters, some in their nightclothes, some carrying small suitcases stuffed with family valuables. Some even took their pets—cats, dogs, and rabbits—in baskets. One woman was carrying a canary in a gold-painted cage.

Not far from our unit was a street bunker. It was an ugly round concrete building on three levels, two above ground, one below. You had to climb a spiral stairway to go up or down to its many compartments. This was where the crowds were heading. Each person had to show the Shelter Warden their place card which gave them their room and seat number—otherwise they weren't let in.

Typical German order!

By now the sky was full of planes and they were dropping canisters of phosphorus. We watched helplessly as some of the phosphorus landed on people running panic-stricken through the streets. It was horrible. Their skins turned bright red like cooked beetroot, water dripped out of their pores, and their faces became gruesome masks with twisted mouths forming silent screams.

Some of these human torches were staggering towards the grey bunker, setting light to others who were hammering with their fists upon the door. The wardens had shut the bunker once it was full. Those locked out were screaming and rushing round in panic, cursing those inside and trying to save their skins.

But there was nowhere to go.

We could also see blocks of flats and shops, full of flames, burning from the roof down. The fire slowly descended through the buildings like a well-lit lift on its way down. It brought with it crashing timbers, toppling walls, and even flaming bodies.

I wondered how my family was.

How was Anna?

Had they all made it to the Winkel in time? Or were they too locked out?

How was Grandad in his flak unit?

He was an unwilling gunner at the best of times. Did he manage to bring any planes down. 'Thou shalt not kill!' he used to mutter. Perhaps he now chose another quotation from the Bible:

'An eye for an eye. A tooth for a tooth.'

17

'Why?'

When we heard the first wave of planes approaching, Erich said firmly, 'The English—in Halifaxes and Wellingtons.'

I strained my ears, trying to catch the sounds.

'Ye-e-sss,' I agreed. 'But there are others too—Stirlings and Lancasters, I think.'

I stared at Erich.

'My God, this is THE BIG ONE!' I said in alarm.

As it turned out, we were both right—and wrong.

The raids continued for nine nights in a row, with everything the RAF could chuck at us. Hundreds and hundreds of planes, thousands and thousands of bombs. And it wasn't only the English; the Americans joined in the 'Smash Hamburg' show too.

Bombs rained down in a deluge as if to wipe us off the map. Every factory and shipyard, every block of flats, every hospital and church, every cinema and park.

And every living thing.

But why? Why? Why? Why?

It didn't make any sense.

Take our Hagenbeck Zoo. It wasn't hit by a stray bomb. It was targeted by four 'blockbuster' blast bombs, sixteen high-explosives and scores of incendiaries. So I read in the newspaper and saw with my own eyes. Many valuable animals were killed outright by the bombing, and others had to be shot. A few wild animals even escaped into the town; the monkeys were the hardest to catch.

Have you ever seen a badly burned animal running amok, rushing panic-stricken through the streets? It's terrible to hear it screaming, almost worse than humans.

Why destroy this world-famous place of research, this children's zoo of wonder and excitement? Did they think we'd set loose lions and tigers in their towns? Invade them on elephants like Hannibal over the Alps? Send crocodiles across the Channel? Or did they think the zoo was the secret HQ of the German High Command? I just can't make it out.

Why kill old men and women, mothers and little children? Why kill their own prisoners-of-war?

Why bomb our old St Nicholas Cathedral or burn down the Ufa-Palast? Why destroy the house where Johannes Brahms was born and composed his famous cradle song?

Martin closed his eyes and began to sing softly, haltingly, beautifully, as tears streamed down his cheeks.

'*Guten Abend, gute Nacht, mit Rosen bedacht . . .* '

After a while he stopped singing and was quiet. Then he murmured, half to himself, 'My mother used to sing that to me when I was little.'

As he wiped his face with his good hand, he continued to mutter, shaking his head, 'How could the English do this?'

The children were silent, confused, moved by Martin's suffering and his pain.

Surely there must be some mistake?

18

Bonzo

As if by fate, the yapping of a dog brought the shed refugees back to earth. There was something unnerving about the yapping, as if the dog had a fishbone caught in its gullet; or maybe it was trying to raise the animal alert: 'Take cover, brothers and sisters. Bombs are no respecter of animal life!'

At first they tried to ignore the noise, hoping the animal would go away. But the dog must have had the same idea as Iris, seeing the shed as shelter. And that might mean humans, food, comfort.

The strangled barking grew closer and closer. The dog seemed to be in pain.

As all eyes watched the doorway, a sandy mongrel poked its shaggy head round the doorpost. It wasn't sure whether to be pleased to see human life, or to run away in fear of a beating. Its yellow-flecked grey eyes blinked uncertainly as it stared dumbly at the dim figures in the far corner; it could make out four, including the black stove.

'Here, boy,' called Tom gently. 'Come on, we won't hurt you.'

The dog sniffed the air warily as if deciding whether they were friend or foe. Then it lifted its tousled head and bayed to the stars like its wolf ancestors. The cry of anguish unsettled the humans, setting their nerves on edge.

It was bad enough having to put up with bombs and planes, wailing, screaming, whirring, exploding. But a dog howling on their doorstep set their teeth on edge. There was something about the baleful look in its wild eyes that suggested the dog wished to communicate. But what?

Every time it howled, it turned its head towards the trees and retreated a couple of paces.

'I think it wants us to follow it,' offered Martin.

Tom edged forward on his knees, slowly approaching the animal, holding out his hand for the dog's inspection. At first the dog backed away; yet steadily curiosity overcame its fear, and it gave a sort of nervous grin. Then it strained its neck forward and took a couple of sniffs at Tom's fingers.

The boy's smell must have satisfied it, for the tone changed from a harsh bark to a pitiful whimper. Finally, it surrendered and gave Tom's hand a welcome lick.

Tom ruffled the fur of its neck, but it leapt back with a pained growl, baring its teeth.

'The poor devil's burned,' said Tom; 'all its neck fur is singed and its back is covered in weals.'

'It must have been caught in a fire,' said Iris. 'Poor old Bonzo.'

With a sharp glance in Martin's direction, she added, 'Apparently Germans bomb animals too.'

Martin frowned. Then, after a pause, he said quietly, 'War spares no one: neither people, nor animals.'

The dog cut short any argument. It howled again, this time at the moon, rolling its eyes towards the railway track and hopping backwards, as if to say, 'Are you stupid or something? Can't you comprehend? Follow me!'

At last the penny dropped.

'Martin's right,' said Tom. 'Bonzo wants us to go with him.'

'Well, we can't,' said Iris firmly. 'We've a prisoner to guard. In any case, we might get ourselves killed. There's an air raid on if you hadn't noticed.'

'Don't worry about me,' said Martin. 'I give you my word to stay put.'

'A German's word can't be trusted,' said Iris.

That riled Martin.

'Oh, so all Germans are liars, are they?' he said. 'That includes German Jews, Communists, and Christians in the Nazi prison camps.'

After a short while, he spoke again.

'If you care so much about animals, think of the poor dog. You British are supposed to be a nation of animal lovers!'

The three shelterers endured an uneasy silence until it was interrupted by the dog who continued its whining and wheezing appeals for help.

The noise was fraying their nerves like a rusty knife cutting through old rope.

'For Pete's sake, Sis,' appealed Tom, 'we've got to do something. There may be someone dying out in the darkness somewhere.'

Iris wasn't sure what to do. Her jaw jutted defiantly but her troubled eyes and twitching hands betrayed her uncertainty. A lull had settled over the city, with just the occasional drone of planes at the margins: over Spithead Fort, round Gosport way, then on to Portchester, past Portsdown Hill, back across Langstone Harbour and round again.

It was like vultures circling their prey.

'I suppose we could make a dash for it before the bombers return to the attack,' she said slowly. 'As long as Bonzo doesn't take us on a wild goose chase.'

'If you're worried about me,' said Martin grumpily, 'I'll come with you. I could do with a breath of fresh air.'

That settled it.

From then on the dog took charge. It led them through the drizzle along the track towards Hilsea Halt. Every so often it would stop, squat on its haunches, swivel its head round and stare at the three stragglers, as if to say, 'Hurry up. We haven't got all night!'

Only Tom was able to walk normally; he had to link

arms with Iris limping along on one side, and Martin stumbling along on the other.

'Isn't there a little cottage by the Halt?' said Iris to Tom as they trudged through the rain. 'The old station master's house?'

'Oh yes, that's right,' he replied. 'Old Ma Figgins lives there as far as I know. The moggy woman.'

She was known as Moggy Figgins because she took in stray cats and dogs. Goodness knows what she fed them on—mice and bird stew, some folk said, and snail and slug pudding.

Even before they rounded the bend in the track, they knew that tragedy lay ahead. They could smell it. They could hear it. They could see an orange glow and dark brown smoke battling with wind and rain. The cottage was plainly on fire, presumably hit by an incendiary bomb. Being made of old ship's timbers, it must have been a veritable tinder box, even when dampened by rain.

They quickened their step as best they could.

As the three of them turned the bend, the full horror of the blaze hit them straightaway. They were plainly too late to save anyone. Blazing blackened beams and smouldering cornerposts were all that was left of the once-pretty little cottage.

It was weird to see straight through the house and out the other side.

They spotted no sign of life.

The heat of the fire brought them to a halt some distance from the cottage. They stood there helplessly, shielding their faces with their arms. The guide dog, his mission accomplished, was running to and fro, gazing fearfully at the burning wreck of his home.

Martin took charge.

'Iris, help me put on my flying helmet and goggles; they're in the pocket of my overalls. I'll try to get as close as I can.'

Iris did as he said. His clothes were likely to be more flame-resistant than hers or Tom's. As Martin bowed his head, she jammed the leather headgear on his head and over his ears, tying it under his chin. Then she stuck the goggles over the helmet, pulling the elastic band down the back.

'There, be careful,' she said, quickly adding, 'We don't want to lose a valuable prisoner.'

Tom and Iris stood at the edge of the track where they were just able to bear the heat. Martin, meanwhile, stepped forward on unsteady legs, his good hand shielding his face. He skirted the house, treading across the little vegetable garden at the back. Through the cracked windows of the kitchen he was able to make out a tiny crumpled figure on the floor; bent sticks of arms curled round what looked like dead rats, all nakedly grey and burnt.

As he was staring at the corpse, he felt a tug at his trouser leg. It was the sandy mongrel, pulling him away and whining, as if to say, 'OK, you've seen it. There's nothing you can do. Come away.'

Martin took a few steps backwards, yet found the dog still tugging at his trouser leg, guiding him towards the lean-to hut at the bottom of the garden. As he drew near, he caught a faint whine from inside. And when he opened the rickety door, he stared in amazement. Then he smiled.

'Well, well, well,' he breathed. 'Wonders will never cease.'

On returning to the children, he gave them a brief description of Moggy Figgins's death.

'But come, I want to show you something,' he said mysteriously.

He led the children into the trees and round the back of the burning cottage. Bonzo was sitting outside the lean-to, looking as pleased as Punch and wagging his tail.

As Martin flung open the door, the children gasped.

On an old blanket lay a black and white dog. She was feeding three sandy-haired pups. All four of them seemed totally unconcerned at the intrusion, the air raid, the fire and the bombs. All that mattered was food.

'Once the raid's over we'll bring the dogs some water and food,' said Iris. 'And we'll tend to Bonzo's wounds. In the morning.'

'If we survive till morning,' said Tom miserably.

'You'll survive,' said Martin. 'And so will your animals.'

They made their way back in silence to the railway shed.

'Funny, isn't it,' said Martin philosophically, 'how one dies as another is born. Death and life. Life and death.'

It was a painful reminder of his family back in Hamburg.

19

The Firestorm

Once back in the shelter, the three prisoners of the night stared forlornly at the continuing blitz. There was clearly no escape—not for a long while, by the look of it. Whether they liked it or not, they were stuck with each other's company.

Both children wanted to hear more about Martin's experiences of war. It was Tom who asked, 'Martin, what happened when the raid was over?'

'It's not a nice story,' said Martin. 'But if you really want to know, I'll tell you all about it.'

The All-Clear went at three o'clock in the morning. It was Sunday 28th July.

But the nightmare was barely beginning. All around us the city was burning and, here and there, fuel tanks and delayed action bombs were exploding, loud enough to burst your eardrums.

The streets all about us were full of soot that clogged the nose and forced its way into ears and mouth. Tears were streaming from our eyes as a result of the incendiaries. As best we could, Erich and I cleaned them with our handkerchiefs dipped in buckets of water left at street corners. And we showed the terrified youngsters in our unit how to stop their eyes smarting.

Now what?

There was no point staying at our post since the planes had all gone home; we had only the moon to fire at. The officer in charge ordered us to form a *Schnellkommando* unit and give help wherever we were needed. That meant Erich and me taking a car and wooden trailer with a couple of fifteen year olds for company. So we drove round the streets looking for someone to help.

But everyone needed help! It was hopeless.

The sights I saw that night will haunt me forever. I wouldn't wish them on my worst enemy.

By now the civilians had left their shelters, eager to find out whether their homes were still standing. There were a few, old folk mainly, who were still indoors, inside their houses, or what was left of them.

At Schaar Market we saw sailors rescuing people from a burning house, passing them down from balcony to balcony. They'd already saved about a dozen when, all at once, the house collapsed like a pack of cards, sending everyone, victims and rescuers, to their deaths. It was a dreadful sight.

Further down the street, at the Big New Market, we came upon another tragedy. An old woman was calling for help from the fourth-floor window of a big house. The room behind her was ablaze. We stopped the car and ran with some men to fetch a ladder. At last we found one long enough to reach the fourth floor, and a couple of firemen climbed up to save the poor woman. But it was no good: the heat and flames drove them back at the second floor. I had a go too and, with a wet rag over my nose and mouth, I made it to within a few steps of her window. I could just touch the woman's outstretched hands with my fingertips.

It was awful. So near and yet so far! I couldn't quite make the last inch. I had to shin back down and watch from below as the woman stared out with wild eyes as if accusing me of abandoning her. All at once, she caught fire and fell back into the flames. Her strangled screams will remain with me forever.

Our throats were parched from the heat, the dust, the smoke, and the phosphorus fumes that still drifted through the streets. I saw a young woman sitting on the pavement nearby, breast-feeding her baby. She was dressed in no more than a ragged nightdress and all her hair was burned away.

Dazed people passed by in a constant stream of misery, unseeing, unfeeling for all but themselves.

When dawn came, no daylight came with it. A thick blanket of smoke was drifting over the city, mainly from the hundreds of fires still unattended. It was a single huge black cloud, very low, like when a thunderstorm descends from the skies in the middle of summer.

The streets were thronged with people clambering over the ruins, some searching for relatives, others looking for pets or valuables they might salvage from the rubble. People were grabbing whatever they could; and many were shell-shocked, not knowing what they were doing.

I came across a little boy, about twelve years old. He had a rucksack on his back with a baby's head poking out of it. When I stopped to talk to him, I discovered that the head was that of his brother. I didn't have the heart to tell him his baby brother was beyond saving.

The worst thing about the bombing was not so much the bombs as the fires they started. When we drove our car and trailer to the top of a hill overlooking the town, we saw an awesome sight. There before us were not isolated fires, but a single blaze. Set in the darkness was a vast dome of bright red fire, like the glowing heart of a volcano. Above the rooftops hovered a misty red haze. I looked down, fascinated, yet horrified. I had never seen a fire like that before. It was one great sea of flame, a *Feuersturm*—firestorm—they called it.

Clearly, if we were to be of any use at all, we needed to get close to the main firestorm area. So we headed along the Süderstrasse towards the centre of town. As we approached, the heat from the surrounding houses was almost unbearable. The two young boys sitting in the open trailer were whimpering and crying. Erich and I were slightly better off in the enclosed car.

Burning people ran and staggered after us, others tried to climb into our trailer, but we had to shake them off and they often remained lying by the wayside. Scores of others were already dead or unconscious in the road. At the junction of Süderstrasse and Louisenweg, our trailer ran into a bomb crater and got stuck fast. So we had to unhitch it and take the boys into the car with us; in the meantime, two other fellows shoved inside and there were now six of us crammed into the car.

After another two hundred yards we were forced to halt behind a burning tramcar; and the heat set fire to our car immediately, forcing us all to hop out swiftly. As we stood there, surrounded by the Fires of Hell, we were sure our end had come. There seemed no way out: no car, no trailer, no path through the wall of flame.

Yet, ironically, it was the firestorm that came to our rescue. I found myself being sucked into an enormous bomb crater in the middle of the road. There was nothing I could do to resist: I just surrendered to the irresistible force.

Erich, myself, and one of the lads slithered feet first down the side, all the way to the bottom. We were engulfed by a deafening noise, like that of an old church organ playing all the notes at once.

That crater saved our lives. Anyone left outside had no chance of survival. The inferno swept over them, drowning the poor devils in a sea of fire.

At the bottom of the crater was a broken water main, gushing water so fast we soon had to fight against the flood. Some people had already drowned or were buried when the sides of the crater caved in. Above us was the searing heat that threatened to consume us, below was the gushing water that threatened to drown us.

Because I was still wearing my driving goggles, I could see everything clearly: burning people being swept past the crater by the firestorm, dead bodies floating by me in the flood, dying victims uttering gurgling cries.

When people die, they first scream, then whimper, and after that comes a death rattle in their throat followed by silence. It isn't a very dignified end.

I don't know how long Erich and I remained in the water. It was about three hours after the terrible firestorm started that it began to die down. Eventually, the wind dropped and within two or three hours the storm had subsided. All the same, the intense heat at the centre of the firestorm remained; it was ages before rescue workers could get through to the hottest parts. That was where we were.

They probably thought there was no hurry since no one could possibly have survived.

I guess it was around midday—it never got light so we couldn't tell the time—that someone came to save us. At first I thought Hamburg had fallen to the enemy, for I was astonished to hear an English voice, shouting down, 'Hold on! Help's coming.'

Through the smoke I could just make out the navy blue jacket of a British POW; I realized this man had been detailed for rescue work. He was a young fellow, obviously a sailor from his shirt. His hands and face were badly burned, but he didn't seem to care for himself as he began hauling survivors out of the crater.

When he pulled me out by my hands, some of his skin stuck to me in shreds. I couldn't help noticing a tattoo on the back of his hand—of a bird, I think. I remember thinking that the tattoo must be quite deep, because it had remained even when the top layers of skin had flaked off.

It must have been sheer agony for him, yet he continued to pull us—the enemy—out, saving our lives. A real hero, that man. Goodness knows what went through his mind at the carnage caused by bombs from his own people.

I left him with a 'Thanks, comrade' in English. But he was too busy to pay any heed.

I set off with Erich in the direction of our old post. The air was barely breathable and my head swam with the smoke I had inhaled. Dead and dying lay everywhere. Most were naked since their clothes had been burnt off. What amazed me was how small the bodies had become: evidently heat shrinks a corpse to half its normal size.

Another odd thing about the dead. They were all lying face down. Only later did we find out that they had died through lack of oxygen; the blast had sucked it out of the air.

Eventually we reached our old searchlight unit; it was now just a heap of smoking rubble containing charred bones and ash. No one was left alive.

20

The Firing Squad

In case of emergency, our orders were to report to the nearest command post. It was only a few blocks away. Not quite true. The post was now three piles of rubble and mangled bodies away. It should still be in one piece since it was in a lead-lined basement deep underground.

The CO was an elderly SS officer whose path I'd crossed once before—not a memorable experience. He knew of Grandad's 'unreliability' and his less than enthusiastic commitment to the cause; he tarred me with the same brush.

So when Erich and I reported to him, he glared up from his desk through steel-framed spectacles. Yet he kept his thin lips sealed. We were kept standing to attention, staring straight ahead; in the meantime, he prowled round us, tapping his cane upon olive green trousers and shiny boots. Now and then, a low growl came from his throat as if he wanted to tear someone apart.

At last, he picked up his black cap with its SS badge on the front, stuck it on his head and stood before me, his face so close I could smell his garlic breath.

'Pohl,' he said ominously, 'I remember you. It's cowards like you who let the enemy get away with murder. But the Führer will make them pay for their crime, I vow to you. We'll wipe the swine off the face of the earth, do you hear?'

I did not respond.

Stepping back a pace to address the two of us, he went on, 'Right, you two will take responsibility for the enemy in our midst. We're short of able-bodied officers; so you'll have to do. Jump to it. I want you to round up all English POWs on the loose. Assemble them at the prison barracks.'

As we gave the Hitler salute and turned on our heel to leave, he called after us, 'We'll teach the swine such a lesson that Churchill's ears will burn. In future he'll think twice about bombing innocent people. Two can play at that game!'

What did he mean about teaching them a lesson? I had to put in a word even if it meant enraging him even more. I turned round in the doorway and said in a respectful voice, 'Herr Hauptmann, forgive me, but Erich and I would not be here if it weren't for an English sailor. He saved our lives by rescuing us from a bomb crater. It's not his fault that we were bombed. After all, they're in the firing line too!'

He smiled grimly.

'That's exactly where I want them!' he muttered. 'Now get going. Heil Hitler!'

There was nothing for it but to carry out orders. For the next couple of hours Erich and I roamed the streets, looking for prisoners of war. They weren't easy to find since they didn't wear regulation uniform or stars on their sleeves, like Jews or gypsies; all they wore was their own naval or army tunic.

Even so, how do you tell one dirty, charred set of rags from another? All we could do was go up to a suspect and ask politely, 'Excuse me, are you English?'

That didn't always work; we got some dusty replies.

'Well, no, old boy, I'm Scottish actually.'

'Certainly not, boyo. I'm as Welsh as the valleys of Cymru.'

Since the SS officer had specified English, we let them go, though we knew full well that by 'English' he meant 'British'.

We were marching about a dozen prisoners along the road when we suddenly came upon the sailor who'd saved our lives. He was sitting by the roadside on an old pram tipped on its side. He was having a quiet smoke, gazing into space through empty eyes. Someone had bandaged his burnt hands, though the white bandages were already grubby and bloodstained.

Going up to him, I said politely, 'Pardon me, you are English, aren't you?' He looked up vacantly; his eyes were tired and bloodshot. He didn't reply straightaway. He just stared through me. Then he spoke quietly, forming each word like a craftsman moulds clay.

'I'm a human being, laddie, a member of the human race. By chance I was born in England, if that's what you mean. At the moment, I feel more German than English, if you can understand that. What inhuman race could commit this terrible crime?'

I felt sick inside. I was having to arrest this noble man, this selfless hero who had risked his life to save me and my fellow Germans. And here I was maybe condemning him to death at the hands of the SS. I couldn't speak.

Erich took the decision for me.

'*Komme, bitte,*' was all he said.

The sailor shrugged, stood up slowly and fell in line.

'War's cruel,' he muttered.

Erich and I led our pitiful column to the POW barracks down by the Elbe. Waiting for us was the SS captain.

'Is this miserable crew all you could find?' he shouted. 'I've seen more monkeys from the zoo about town than this lot!'

'Most prisoners died in the bombing, Herr Hauptmann,' I said. 'They weren't allowed into the bunkers.'

He gave me a sour look, suspecting treachery. But there was little he could do—other than go hunting prisoners himself. And he didn't speak any English.

'Right,' he said. 'We'll make an example of these pigs.'

Pointing to Erich, he ordered, 'Kastner, I want all POWs on the parade ground. Right now! They'll learn that Germans pay their debts.'

Turning to me, his tone changed to a vicious snarl, 'You, Pohl, line the English up against the barrack wall.'

Only then did I fully realize what he meant by paying debts. He was going to shoot the prisoners!

If that wasn't bad enough, his next words hit me in the face like a rifle butt.

'You will execute them!'

I couldn't help myself. I blurted out, 'That's not fair. It's against the Geneva Convention. It's inhuman. It's—'

'Who said war was fair?' he asked, giving me one of his superior smiles. 'The cold-blooded murder of women and children isn't fair, is it? The burning of babies isn't fair, is it? This isn't a game of football, you know; fair play isn't in the rules.'

His tone abruptly changed again.

'You will do as I say!' he shouted. 'As a member of the Hitler Youth you will obey orders without question. You hope to be a pilot, don't you? Well, our Luftwaffe takes only obedient officers with *my* blessing. Bear that in mind!'

By this time Erich was leading out a ragged group of POWs—Russians and Poles, French and Belgians, the war orphans without home or Fatherland. About three hundred in all. They made a pitiful sight— skinny, haggard, with sunken eyes and sallow cheeks. Some of the faces were like death masks, bearing no sign of life.

Being prisoners was misery enough. Being the bombing target of their own comrades had destroyed all belief in humankind. Like the condemned English prisoners, they were mostly past caring about their fate.

While this ragged riff-raff shuffled into columns on the parade ground, the SS captain barked orders to the thirteen English men. I had to translate, adding a 'please' and 'thank you' to soften the blow.

At first the prisoners stared, uncomprehending. Why? What had they done to deserve execution? They had only helped Germans in distress . . .

But they knew from experience that pleas for clemency would fall on deaf ears. So, with bowed heads and hunched shoulders, they walked slowly towards the brick wall at one end of the barrack square, like a trickle of rainwater approaching a drain—about to disappear forever.

The SS captain clearly wanted to savour his big moment.

'Pohl, follow me,' he snapped.

He marched smartly over to the condemned prisoners, came to attention and turned to me.

'First translate, then shoot,' he said.

'English prisoners-of-war,' he began. 'Your countrymen have broken all conventions of war by their mass bombing of innocent civilians. You will pay for this barbaric act. The German nation will fight with renewed vigour to avenge this crime. Led by our great Führer, we will not only win the war, we will march into England and hang your war criminals!'

He paused to let his words sink in through my translation. Not a flicker of emotion showed on the men's faces.

'You men will pay for your nation's crime,' he continued. 'Your punishment is death. That is all.'

When I finished my translation, one or two men looked up in surprise. They seemed unable to take in the verdict. Was this really to be their last moment on earth?

The sailor with bandaged hands stepped forward. He spoke calmly, without rancour or fear.

'Kill us, if you wish. But remember this: you're sinking to the same level as the bombers.'

As I translated, he stepped back into line, right at the end. He seemed resigned to being shot.

The captain said nothing. Taking his pistol from its holster, he held it out to me.

'Use your own gun, Pohl,' he said. 'Aim for the middle of the forehead. Start on the right with that insolent sailor. When you run out of bullets, take my Luger and finish off the rest.'

What was I to do?

How could I kill these men in cold blood?

I stood there dumbly, arms dangling at my side. A lead weight seemed to stop my hand rising to the pistol holster. Although the POWs had not followed the conversation, they were taking a keen interest in my dilemma.

I searched for the eyes of the sailor on the right. But he gave no message, just stared down at his feet. I had to take the decision myself: my conscience or my duty?

No! I couldn't do it. It wasn't right.

I was well aware of the punishment for disobedience. And it wasn't long in coming.

'Will you fire or not?' the captain shouted.

I turned slowly to face him and, with shaking voice, I said, 'I cannot kill innocent men, Herr Hauptmann.'

He half expected that answer, I'm sure. He had been disobeyed in front of hundreds of witnesses. Now he had to assert his authority. For all to hear he bellowed out, 'Pohl, join the prisoners! I will shoot you first, personally, for disloyalty to the Führer!'

Head bent, I walked to the side of the English sailor. Do you know how it feels to die at seventeen? Panic, despair, disbelief.

All at once a rough bandaged hand squeezed mine and a voice at my side said loudly, 'Well done, laddie. Be brave. Shoulders back, chest out, head high!'

I did as he said and stared straight ahead.

All the while, Erich and the mass of prisoners had been looking on in dumb confusion. Now the situation was clear and they realized we were to be shot.

Suddenly, a lone voice rang out like a shot across the parade ground. It was Erich's.

'*Nein!*'

Almost at once it was followed by other shouts:

'*Non!*'

'*Nee!*'

'*Njet!*'

'*Ne!*'

'No, no, no!'

The startled SS officer swivelled round. To his amazement, the POWs led by Erich were advancing towards him. The right hand holding the pistol wavered uncertainly. To shoot or not to shoot? He was beginning to fear for his own life.

God knows what would have happened had not fate—or British bombers—intervened.

Right at that moment the siren sounded. It cut the tension like a knife. Not only did it save the captain's face, it saved his bacon—and ours—too.

'I'll deal with you later,' he cried in a strangled voice. 'Back to the barracks!'

We never saw him again. Whether he was killed in the second round of bombing, or just vanished into the maelstrom of war, I'll never know.

Fortunately, the incident was forgotten—or covered up—and we condemned men survived.

21

'Ginger'

When Martin finished speaking, a stifling silence filled the hut. And noises from outside came flooding in: exploding bombs, droning planes, driving rain. Somehow the children had blocked out the present to hear the past. Now that the source had run dry, the sounds of night rushed in to fill the void.

Yet images of Martin's story crowded out anxiety for their safety. Both children's minds kept returning to the past, mulling over the horror.

It was terribly confusing. If Martin was telling the truth—and no one could surely invent such scenes—it upset all they had heard about the war. They felt cheated.

Someone was lying.

Not that they had sympathy for Hitler or his cut-throat Nazi gang. They had caused the war in the first place.

But people are people. Not all Germans were bad. Little children hadn't done anything wrong—so why kill them? Animals in the zoo weren't harming anyone—so why bomb them to bits? Old people, mothers, and young girls weren't soldiers at the front—so why slaughter and maim them?

Wasn't it cold, calculated murder?

They had no answers to Martin's 'Why?'.

Then there was Martin's heroism in trying to save the English POWs who, in turn, had saved his life. He had been ready to sacrifice his young life for them.

What a topsy-turvy war it was. Not at all as simple as they had been led to believe: Goodies versus Baddies.

Yet there was a more personal concern uppermost in

Iris's mind. She had to bring it out into the open,
though she didn't know how.

'Martin,' she began uncertainly.

When nothing followed, Martin realized she needed
help.

'Yes, Iris, please, anything. What can I tell you? What
is it?'

She couldn't get it out.

'Oh, thank you for being so frank,' she said meekly.
'It must be very painful for you. War is terrible, isn't
it?'

'Yes,' he said thoughtfully. 'War is truly terrible.'

He realized she wished to say more; something was
bothering her. But it had to come in her own time,
without coaxing.

'War is just as tragic for civilians in Portsmouth as it
is in Hamburg,' he continued. 'A German life is as
precious as an English life. A German bomb dropped on
children is just as cruel as an English bomb that takes
away young lives. Innocent victims of war share a
common grief.'

He talked on until Iris had summoned enough courage
to put her question.

'Martin,' she said once more in a faltering voice. 'That
English sailor you met . . . Could you tell us more about
him?'

'Well, to tell the truth, I don't remember much about
his appearance—apart from his hands. Why are you so
interested in him?'

Iris's voice was breaking as she tried to form the words.

'I think . . . it may have been . . . our . . . dad!'

Martin didn't want to hurt her feelings. It was
impossible, of course: the coincidence was too great.
She was clutching at straws, hoping her father had
survived. And yet . . . War did sometimes throw up
surprises. The least he could do was listen.

'What makes you think that?' he asked gently.

It was Tom who provided an answer.

'Mum told us Dad may have been taken prisoner when his ship sank in the English Channel.'

'A friend recognized him by the tattoo,' added Iris; 'a little dove on the back of his hand. He had it done just after war broke out—his 'dove of peace' he called it. It was his lucky charm, meant to keep him safe.'

Martin cast his mind back to the grim-faced prisoner-of-war who had saved his life and whom he'd joined among the condemned. Yes, he could see the tattoo even now—it might well have been a dove, dark blue ink upon red raw skin.

'As far as I can recall,' he said slowly, 'the tattoo may have been a dove. It was on the back of his right hand, between thumb and forefinger.'

He didn't want to build false hopes. It's true, if survivors were taken prisoner in the Channel, they could have gone to Hamburg to work in the shipyards, probably on U-boats.

'But there must be a lot of sailors with tattoos—most, I should think,' he said.

'Yes, of course,' said Tom resignedly.

But Iris wasn't going to let it drop so easily.

'Is there anything else you remember?'

'Not really,' he said truthfully.

Then a vague picture of the man's face flashed before his eyes and he gave a start. Good God, there was something that had struck him at the time. Martin stared hard at the children; but the darkness veiled his view. He need not have bothered. For he had seen a clear likeness that linked them to his rescuer. Almost the first thing he noticed when he had come to and seen Iris leaning over him was her long hair.

It was red.

Gold burnished by the sun, he had thought feverishly at the time. Tom too had an unruly mop of ginger hair above a freckled face.

'I do remember the man had ginger hair,' Martin said.

It evoked no response apart from a gasp, as if an upward gush of air had caught in their throats.

He felt uneasy at the children's silence.

'Did your dad have red hair?' he asked hesitantly. 'Not that it necessarily proves anything,' he added quickly.

'His friends used to call him "Ginger",' said Tom.

Iris murmured, as if afraid of the reply, 'Have you any idea what happened to him?'

'None at all, I'm afraid,' said Martin. 'Erich and I were in too much of a hurry to get away from the firing squad. We dashed back to the first command post we could find. The last I saw he was standing, watching us disappear. He was waving farewell.

'If it *was* your dad, you can be proud of him. Tell your mother he's a real hero.'

The children fell silent again. And all three returned to the deadly firework display beneath the leaden sky. Yet it no longer held their full attention. Each of them felt somehow tied together by the single thread from the children's father.

After a while, Tom asked, 'Martin, will you tell us about your family and the girl in the photo. What happened to them?'

Martin sighed deeply and did not reply. He had leaned back against the wooden wall, closed his eyes and evidently fallen asleep. He was trying to summon up the courage to describe the most painful part of his story. It was some time before he opened his eyes and began to speak, quietly, in a shaking voice.

22

Trapped

After the second round of bombing Erich and I parted
company: he went in search of his family, I in search of
mine. We went in sombre mood, having seen the total
destruction with our own eyes. Although we didn't say
so, we knew there was not much hope of their survival.

By my reckoning, Gretchen and Grandma would have
had time to reach the Winkel after the siren went.
That's where I should find them if they were still alive.

It was tough going and very dangerous, what with
houses collapsing and fire suddenly shooting out as from
a flamethrower's gun. In places the heat was unbearable,
and I had to hold a wet hanky over my nose and mouth.
It was as if the air had been sucked out and the streets
sealed in a box lined with a leaden skylid slammed down
tight.

The summer trees were stripped of leaves and
branches; some were dragged out of the ground by the
roots. I had to watch out for fiery whirlwinds that could
snatch a person off the street and turn him into a human
torch while others, just a few yards away, were
completely untouched. To avoid catching fire, I doused
myself with buckets of water which still stood in pails
outside houses. The wind was so strong in places that it
forced doors of houses open and broke windows. And it
was accompanied by clouds of sparks, resembling a
blizzard of red snowflakes. Added to that, the wind
shrieked and howled as it raced through the streets.

Where houses had stood only a few hours before,
single walls with empty windows now towered upwards.
In between were great heaps of smoking rubble, still
glowing. Torn overhead wires hung down everywhere.

I had to pass Grandad's church and our house on the way to the shelter; it was no surprise to see the house gone. Oddly, the wall between the dining room and the staircase was still standing; I could see the dresser and I remember wondering where was my beloved Meissen porcelain figure of a shepherd and dog that ought to be standing on it.

Yet the old grey-stone church was still standing, battered but unbowed.

I didn't hang around gawking as the soles of my feet were burning—I was afraid of bursting into flame at any moment.

Finally, I reached the top of Hammer Landstrasse and stared about me, confused. Where was the Winkel? It should have been here, grey and solid, in the middle of the road. Had someone moved it to a safer spot? But how can you shift a big brick shelter?

Before me was a crater full of dark-red broken bricks. Not a sign of a living thing except a brown and white dog with a stupidly long tail; it was sniffing at the ruins.

'Hans! Here, boy.'

When I called his name, our old guard dog came running up, clearly relieved at finding something familiar in this upside-down world. His big brown eyes looked at me as if to say, 'Martin, what on earth is going on?'

I could only ruffle the brown fur on his neck, asking him, 'Where are they, Hans? Where's Mum, Grandma, Gretchen?'

He had no answer either.

As I stood there, dazed, I noticed our neighbour's sixteen-year-old daughter, Margret, shuffling towards me. If she was safe, perhaps my family was safe too. They would have shared the same bunker.

Margret looked an awful sight. She was wearing a charred army greatcoat several sizes too big for her; her hair was singed to the roots, her face was black and scarred by ugly red weals, her hands were all burned.

'Come,' she said quietly, 'let's find somewhere safe, so we can talk.'

I followed her down to the river where we found a bench to sit on and talk. She told me her story.

'When the siren went,' she said, 'we hurried to the shelter. It was all very orderly; some of us sat on the floor where we thought it would be safer, heads bowed, praying and waiting for the bombs to drop. When they did, the earth shook, the walls cracked and the plaster came down like flour until the whole bunker was one big cloud of dust.

'It was like an earthquake. No one spoke a word. And then this girl suddenly started to laugh; her nerves had snapped. Someone told her it was no laughing matter, but she just cried, "This is all I ever wanted." She really had no idea what she was saying.

'We could hear this hail of bombs all around us; and our bunker went up and down like a lift—yet we found out later that we were only being hit by incendiary bombs and phosphorus. All the same, our candles went out, glass shattered, the door was ripped off its hinges and smoke seeped into the shelter through every crack.

'The flickering light of many fires lit up the bunker; the heavens were raining fire. The air outside the door was filled with flames. It would surely have meant certain death to leave our shelter. Then a storm started, a shrill howling in the street. It grew into a hurricane so that we had to abandon all hope of fighting the fire creeping up on us. The entire street, the canal, as far as we could see, was just one massive sea of flame.

'Word of what was happening in the street must have spread to the people at the back of the shelter because they broke down the wall separating the bunker from the other end of the street. That was a tragic mistake for they found themselves staring into a furnace. Since the bunker door was half off its hinges, with the air being drawn out of the bunker, smoke and fire came pouring through the gap in the wall.

'All of us began to cough and choke. Through the dense smoke I could hear people screaming, but this faded away to hoarse gasping. I guess they were suffocating.

'I knew we were within seconds of death. I could not speak to my mother because of my gas mask. So I tapped her on the shoulder as a sign that I was going to try to get out—a few seconds more and I would have had it. I thought she would follow.

'I waited for a moment when no burning debris was falling, then I sprang out into the street and started to run against the wind. I headed for a small park down the road where I might find safety.

'Flying sparks of phosphorus were burning my hands. I had on this old army coat and I pulled it over my head. I ran eighty or a hundred yards to a railway bridge which I had to pass under to reach the park. But it was one mass of flames with what looked like tailor's dummies blocking the way.

'Panic gave me strength. I counted, "One, two, three!" and dashed through the wall of fire, trying to avoid slipping on the dead bodies and the fat of molten corpses running over the tarmac.

'I made it, without any serious burns. Only my shoes and hair were singed. I ran blindly on and managed to reach the park where I found a small ticket kiosk, miraculously untouched by the fire. I squeezed inside and spent the rest of the night there.

'I never found my mother and was never sure how she died. I feel guilty about abandoning her; I thought she was following me. But she wasn't. I never met another survivor from the Winkel.'

I asked Margret whether all my family was in the bunker.

'If the fire didn't kill them, the bomb did,' she

replied. 'The Winkel took a direct hit straight after I'd fled—but they must have all been dead by then. Wait a minute: your grandma wasn't there. I recall your mum saying your grandpa was on duty and that she'd had to leave the stubborn old woman at home, clutching her Bible.'

I left Margret on the riverbank and made my way back to the ruins of our house. Dust was everywhere, clogging my nose and mouth. All that remained was a single wall; the rest was smouldering rubble. Yet as I clambered over the twisted wood and stone, I thought I heard a knocking.

Frantically I began to clear away stones and bricks. I had no tools to aid me; I worked with my bare hands, chucking aside the small pieces, rolling the larger ones out of the way. By now it was growing light and a beautiful blue sky streaked with smoke-grey clouds gleamed above me. My hands hurt. My eyes smarted. Yet I dug and dug.

All at once, a hand appeared, bloody and dusty. A moment later I saw a second hand. Still warm! I carefully dug out the arms. Then I gripped the hands and pulled. Dirt slithered after them, but the weight upon the body held it back. Desperately I enlarged the hole, then started to pull again.

I uncovered a dusty grey face, eyes closed, cuts on the cheeks.

I dug deeper, deeper. Now I found a torso in a torn black dress—her 'Sunday best'. Deeper. Below the knees were smashed legs, feet crushed to a bloody, dust-encrusted mass.

'She's dead,' I heard someone say. 'They're all dead.'

It was Erich. I hadn't heard him approach. As we sat down in the rubble of what was once my childhood home, Erich told me what he'd found.

'I ran into a fellow, Gunther, who lived nearby, a bit younger than us. He told me the whole sorry story.

They couldn't have suffered much. He said he was sheltering in the same basement as my family when a bomb fell and the building caught fire. When the door of the basement started to burn, they all decided to get out rather than be roasted alive.

'It was like a ring of fire at the circus through which animals have to jump. He and his Aunt Emma and mother just made it in time before the whole building collapsed.

'He ran through the rain of sparks blowing down the street, pushing into the wind. The plan was to make for a piece of open ground on the other side of the canal, about two hundred yards away. But they couldn't cross the street to it since the asphalt had melted. There were people in the roadway, some already dead, some still alive, lying there, but stuck in the molten asphalt. They must have rushed into the road without thinking and got stuck; now they were on their hands and knees screaming for help.

'The only way to the canal was down a steep bank. Gunther and his family linked hands and started to roll down; it was too steep to get down any other way. He lost contact with his mother and aunt, rolled over dead bodies, and finally found himself beside the canal. He soaked himself in the water which eased his burns. He had lost his mother and aunt. No one else survived.'

In one night, Erich and I had lost everyone: our mothers, grandmothers, sisters, and friends.

But what of Grandad?

23

Grandad's Story

Erich and I were drawn like a magnet to Grandad's church. It stood like a wounded warrior amid the chaos of the battlefield. Its stained-glass windows had shattered, its roof was full of more holes than a pepper pot, its oak doors reeled back, blasted inwards. Yet the grey stone walls stood firm and defiant.

'The wise man builds his house upon the rock.'

We entered through the blasted oak doors and at once felt at home. It was good to exchange the unfamiliar smells of the street for the familiar must and polish of our own church.

Where the outside grass and trees lay scorched and bare, here Mother's big bronze urns of roses breathed the freshness of Nature's innocence. Three rows of black numbers high above the pulpit announced last Sunday's hymns, and a solitary long candle flickered on the altar.

We had assumed the place empty. Yet someone must have lit the candle; that someone was kneeling before the altar, weeping softly, talking to his God, asking questions.

Erich and I did not wish to intrude upon the man's private grief; we had enough problems of our own. So we sat in a pew at the back, praying for the souls of our family, for Grandad's safety, for our future, for Germany.

After several minutes, the grieving figure pulled itself up on stiff legs and stood, grey head bowed, before Jesus on the cross. Joseph before his crucified son.

I gasped. It was Grandad. I wanted to call out, yet something stopped me: would he want me to witness his tears? Sometimes you need to grieve alone, lost in your own suffering. At that moment, the old man turned and walked slowly, shoulders hunched, eyes downcast, up the stone-flagged aisle. He moved with measured tread, like a mourner at a funeral. I could no longer hide.

As he approached, I stood up and walked unsteadily towards him. We didn't speak. We just hugged one another, sobbing unashamedly on each other's shoulders, wetting each other's cheeks with our tears. It was a good five minutes before Grandad pulled away, wiped his eyes and spat out one word, 'War!'

Then, seeing Erich, he pulled himself together and gave a wry smile.

'Dear, oh dear, God knows, I'm Pastor with a duty to comfort others in their hour of need; yet I've no one to comfort me!'

Staring at the floor, he said quietly, with such pain in his eyes, 'They're all dead, God rest their souls.'

I wasn't sure whether it was a question or a statement. But I told him all I knew and how I'd found Grandma's body.

'Stubborn old biddy!' he muttered with a tinge of pride, as if the rough phrase would conceal his grief.

The three of us sat in a row on the shiny oak pew, relating experiences. Grandad's story was no less terrible than ours. What surprised me was how this kindly man of God, who had had to struggle with his conscience even to shoot his gun, had become so bitter, so full of hatred. I listened in shock and horror.

'After the raid, I was sent to help phosphorus-burn victims on the square along the Heidenkampsweg, down by the quay.

'A steamer was waiting to evacuate them up the Elbe. It was my first personal experience of the full horror of war. Many who were burning jumped blindly into the river; people burned to death in terrible pain, some went crazy.

'We had to grade the victims with a label round the neck, giving personal details and their degree of burns. A doctor told me that the larger the area of burn, the less pain people feel, yet the more likely they are to die. When the burns cover a certain portion of the body, death is inevitable.

'This doctor went up and down the rows of victims; those with too much burn he left behind on the quay. There was only room on board for those with a chance of survival. Those abandoned knew they were doomed. One man dragged himself up my leg to get at my pistol—it was awful. I had to fight him off. May God forgive me, I was glad to get away.

'Next day the square was empty. Goodness knows what happened to them.

'I was detailed to aid people still trapped in what was left of Sievekingsallee. The four-storey blocks of flats were just glowing mounds of stone from top to bottom. All I could do was bring out the dead, or what was left of them. Everything seemed to have melted and congealed in one slippery mass.

'Women and children were so charred as to be unrecognizable as human beings. What a terrible death they must have had.

'Little children and babies lay like fried eels on the pavement. Even in death they showed signs of how they must have suffered—their hands and arms cradled their little heads to protect themselves from the heat.

'While I was doing this gruesome work, a group of SS men drove up in a truck. They jumped out smartly and lined up, in full uniform and jackboots, as if on parade. The officer ordered me and the medical orderlies into the truck; we were needed to tend to wounded SS men.

'The man was so arrogant, so unmindful of civilian deaths around us, it made my blood boil. I lost my temper and shouted at him: "Clear off, you arrogant

Nazi! This isn't the time for your SS parades! Go and find someone else to do your dirty work!"

'It was only the fact that I was a priest that saved me from arrest. The officer was so stunned, he turned on his heel and ordered his men back in the truck; and they drove off.

'Soon after, I was walking through burning streets on my way home when I suddenly saw a young girl. It could so easily have been my own granddaughter. She came running towards me. Her face was black with soot except for two streams of tears running down her face. She was dragging her little dead brother behind her over the cobblestones; the right side of his face was scraped raw. She told me she had been wandering about for three days and nights.

'This little girl put her arm round my neck, begging me to take her and her brother with me. All I could do was lead her to the nearest first-aid station. By then I was so angry I would have shot any enemy airmen who had parachuted down. God help me, so I would!'

Grandad took a deep breath before passing a final judgement.

'I would willingly take my place upon the cross if I could have those murderers Hitler and Churchill nailed beside me!'

I had never seen him in such a temper.

24

Flight

Erich, ever the practical one, broke in to change the subject. If any SS had overheard Grandad cursing Hitler, he would have been arrested and even shot, priest or not. This was wartime!

'Pastor,' he said, 'what should we do now?'

Grandad immediately calmed down and put his arm round Erich's shoulders, as if to thank him for changing the subject.

'Well,' he said, 'there doesn't seem much point in hanging around here. We can only bury bodies, not save them. And the soldiers reckon there'll be more raids—though God knows what's left to bomb. The civilian population is to be evacuated to other towns and villages inland. Those who can walk have to make their own way.'

Waving his arm behind him, he then said, 'I've a workshop out the back where I keep an old handcart, a bicycle, and a store of emergency rations. We can take whatever we can salvage from the ruins of our houses, right?'

He looked both of us in the eye, as if noticing the sorry state we were in for the first time.

'Oh, dear, what am I thinking of! You'd better come through to the vestry first; you could both do with a wash and brush-up, get some food inside you and take a rest. We'll set off early tomorrow morning, hoping to God we get through the night safely.'

It was only when he mentioned food that I realized how ravenous I was. I couldn't remember when I'd last eaten or drunk.

When we'd cleaned up and eaten some black bread

and sausages, washed down with what Grandad called his 'holy water'—though it tasted more like 'firewater' sent up from Hell—Erich ran off to see if he could rescue some possessions from his bombed house. He was soon back, pushing an old pram full of blankets, pillows, a kettle, some crockery, photos, meat and cheese and some bottles of cider.

We made up beds on the wooden pews and slept the sleep of the dead, not even waking to the siren or fresh waves of bombers.

As soon as it was light, Grandad woke us with mugs of hot coffee and hunks of bread and cheese. After a quick prayer for a safe journey, we set off. Erich pushed the pram, I pulled the cart and Grandad shoved the heavily-laden bicycle.

We tried to find a safe route, near the canal where the houses were more widely spaced and we didn't have to skirt too much rubble. Fires were still burning here and there. We merged with the human throng, pushing bicycles and handcarts—all weighed down with pitiful possessions. Many people were in their nightclothes, often half burned, with sometimes a coat thrown over their shoulders.

Firemen, soldiers, women and children all mingled together in a silent, stunned mass, with faces blank and uncomprehending.

We passed one man who had lost his senses. He was standing on a mound of bricks from a collapsed wall, holding a swastika flag in one hand and hurling bricks with the other. He was screaming abuse at the fugitives at the top of his voice. When Grandad went up and yelled back at him, he was so stunned, he let us pass.

We continued past bomb craters, over the ruins of collapsed house fronts, by blazing fires. Finally, we reached the town boundary at Wandsbek. Although there were signs of bombing everywhere, the dense clouds of smoke were behind us and the day was becoming clearer. Our stream had now run into the great sea of fugitives on the Lübeck road; a ragged mass of humanity was creeping along under the hot sun.

Each village we came to was full to bursting; farmers gave out hot drinks and milk, but what could they do for thousands of people? As evening approached, we were utterly exhausted and could go no further; our feet were full of blisters. There were no beds, no barns, no stables. Like most others, we just had to lie down beneath the stars. First we filled our kettle from a stream, lit a fire and had supper.

Was this the end?

For many Hamburg people, it was the beginning of the end. The raids came as a shock and undermined their great faith in ultimate victory; it had been this firm belief in victory that had sustained them through previous bad times.

But it was not the END. Far from it.

The army was still in control of much of our great empire and was far from defeat on the battlefield.

If anything, the bombing of Hamburg redoubled the will to fight. The cruelty of the raids drew people together as never before. For the first time, with English help, the Nazis achieved their aim of a united Germany. Even waverers like Grandad, who had never supported the Nazis, were determined to fight back. As for Erich and me, at the first opportunity we reported to a Luftwaffe base, took our flying tests and, within three months, were on our first flying mission to England.

We may not have succeeded, but there are thousands of young people to follow. And maybe through such people we shall yet win the war.

25

The Bomb

As Martin was speaking, the children's attention abruptly switched to their own air raid. They could clearly hear the drone of a single plane coming closer and closer. It dawned on Iris that the railway line to London could be the target; that meant they were in grave danger.

Whether it was the terrible scenes of bombing in Martin's story that finally shattered their nerves no one could say. But when a strong blast rattled the wooden shed and stove, Tom began to cry, first in quiet sobs, then in hysterical wailing that shook his entire body. Iris was on the verge of tears herself.

No storytelling could calm them now. War—and possible death—were far too close.

When Martin took Iris's hand, she hardly noticed— otherwise she would probably have snatched it away. But the strong hand comforted her. And when he took it away to squeeze Tom's arm, she edged closer to him for protection.

The three of them huddled together in the corner.

No one spoke. No one wondered whose side they were on. For the moment, faced by common danger, they were as one. Once the raid was over, everything could return to normal.

The bomb that fell beside the railway track announced its coming with a long-drawn-out scream. They heard it long before it exploded—growing louder and louder and louder, until it almost split their eardrums.

In the blast that followed, the wooden shed was blown

to pieces and swallowed up in a ball of fire. All that
remained was a pile of charred timber and twisted iron.

Later that day, rail inspectors came to check the
damage to the line. They were in for a shock.

'Hey, Jack,' yelled one of the two men. 'Come over
here. Some tramp must have used the old hut as home.
There's a body in the wreckage.'

'Young fellow, too, by the look of him,' said Jack,
coming up.

Under the heap of criss-crossed planks lay a body in
scorched blue overalls and brown leather boots. The
man was spreadeagled on his face upon the ground.
There was no sign of life.

'We'd better go and make out a report,' sighed Jack.
'Bally nuisance, eh?'

As the men moved away, they were startled by a
whimpering noise behind them. It was like a puppy
whining softly. The strange sounds seemed to be coming
from beneath the dead body.

'Blimey! Did you hear that, Danny?' cried Jack in a
shaking voice. 'There must be something, or someone
. . . alive beneath the corpse!'

The two men started tearing away timbers from the
half-buried body. When at last they turned over the fair-
haired man, they reeled back in amazement, unable to
believe their eyes.

Two young children, a boy and a girl, lay trembling
underneath. Apart from shock and scratches, neither
seemed to have come to any serious harm. It was a
miracle.

'Well, well, well,' said Danny slowly, whistling
through his teeth. 'That young fellow gave his life to
save those kiddies.'

'A true hero,' said Jack.

'More than you'll ever know,' came a girl's voice.

Iris was kneeling beside Martin, stroking the fair hair
of her dead prisoner.

Her brother, Tom, slowly got to his feet, brushing dust and debris from his hair. As he gazed at Martin's still figure, tears streamed down his grief-stricken face.

In one hand he still clutched the dead airman's black leather wallet. It was now more precious to him than any souvenir of war.

POSTSCRIPT

Bare Facts

Over 45,000 people were killed in the bombing of Hamburg in July 1943;

A total of 60,595 civilians were killed in German raids on Britain throughout the war;

As many as 50,000 people were killed in British-American raids on the German city of Dresden on 13–14 February 1945—some of them Allied POWs;

85,000 people were killed by US bombers in the raid on the Japanese capital Tokyo on 9–10 March 1945;

118,000 people were killed by the atomic bomb dropped by the USA on the Japanese city of Hiroshima in 1945.

Other Oxford books by James Riordan

Sweet Clarinet

ISBN 0 19 271795 2

Shortlisted for the Whitbread Children's Book Award

I would gladly have welcomed death with a passion—as long as it stopped the pain. 'Oh, God, let me die, please, please, let me die. I'll say my prayers every night, honest, if only you let me die.'

Billy thought growing up in wartime was fun: the fiery skies, exploding factories, the noise of the blitz, playing among the rubble of the bombed houses. But then a bomb fell directly on the shelter where Billy and his mother had gone to escape the bombardment and changed Billy's life for ever.

Billy wakes up in hospital, horribly burned and longing for death—angry at a world in which he will always be a freak, an object of horror or pity, an outcast—until a precious gift from a soldier who is also disfigured gives him hope and a reason for living.

'a deserving contender for the Whitbread Children's Book Prize . . . [a] bitter-sweet story . . . '
Sunday Telegraph

The Young Oxford Book of Football Stories

ISBN 0 19 274179 9

'Some people say football's a matter of life and death. That's ridiculous. It's far more important than that!'

Bill Shankly

This is a collection of stories and poems about the greatest game in the world. They will make you laugh, will make you cry, will make you hold your breath. They're all written by keen football fans such as Michael Parkinson, Barry Hines, Michael Rosen, Robert Swindells and many more. You'll find games which are not decided till the last minute, matches where the winners get shot; girls, boys, dogs, grandfathers, all doing their best, all united by a love of something that's more than a game.

King Arthur

ISBN 0 19 274176 4

Illustrated by Victor G. Ambrus

He clung to the edge of the sky like a tear in the eye of the storm. Then he was falling and darkness enclosed him. Only the bright glow of a sword, held out before him like a torch, lit up his path.

Thus began his dream which was to encompass four centuries. And through his dream came Merlin's words: 'One day, Arthur, you will be king. You will unite this troubled land.'

This is the story of a boy who was born surrounded by danger and magic. Pursued by the black-hearted Vortigern, who had poisoned his father, the little boy escapes in the arms of the magician, Merlin, down a secret path in the darkness. They journey by sea till they come to a mysterious valley. And there he grows up, waiting for his hour to come, waiting to become king.

In this new retelling of the Arthurian legend, James Riordan's resonant and original style is complemented by Victor Ambrus's brilliant recreations of the lost world of King Arthur.

Gulliver's Travels

ISBN 0 19 274178 0

Illustrated by Victor G. Ambrus

'The story I am about to tell is true. My name is Lemuel Gulliver and on the 4th of May 1699 I set sail from Bristol bound for the South Seas.'

Originally written in 1726 as an adult satire, *Gulliver's Travels* has become a classic of children's literature. In this new adaptation, James Riordan has captured the pace and excitement of the original, while preserving much of the bite of Swift's language, including the remark that 'Englishmen are the nastiest race of odious little vermin that ever walked upon the surface of the earth'.

The distinguished artist, Victor Ambrus, has brought vividly to life the two contrasting worlds: the miniature world of Lilliput where Gulliver is drawn on a trolley by a thousand of the King's horses; and the land of the giants, Brobdingnag, where Gulliver has to contend with enormous rats, flies, and eagles. His masterly pictures recreate for children the strange and wonderful world of Gulliver's Travels.